A DAY IN THE LIFE OF STRANGERS

HARPER BLACK

ISBN (paperback): 979-8-9880768-1-0
ISBN (ebook): 979-8-9880768-0-3

Harper Black Writes, LLC

Books may be purchased for educational, business, or sales promotional use.

Chapter 1

Baleigh Emerson has had bad days before, but today was one of those days she was struggling to keep her emotions under control. She'd woken up out of sorts, and the day continued with that same vibe. What followed was a grueling meeting with a temperamental client. In her line of work as a health systems consultant, she dealt with many personality types, but this one was probably the worst she'd had in a long while. Her client, Sally Jensen, was the CEO of Baytown Healthcare and was not having a very good year. The organization was in shambles, and two of its three hospitals were on the verge of losing their accreditation. This was due to the mounting number of patient safety issues, mismanagement of resources, and poor decision-making. The health system's board of directors hired Giles and Associates, the consulting firm Baleigh worked for, to make suggestions on necessary improvements to reverse its downward spiral. Baleigh had a sneaking suspicion that after Baytown Healthcare was once again on solid ground, Jensen's position as CEO would be in jeopardy. After all, this was her mess, and she should not be allowed the benefit of its recovery. Along with righting the ship that was Baytown Healthcare, Baleigh suspected they were also planning to fire the current CEO.

During the horrible meeting, Baleigh reported the findings of her investigation of the health system's operations to a very displeased board. Ms. Jensen was not happy with the report, and rather than let Baleigh finish, she attempted to hijack the meeting and downplay the issues. However, the board chairman was not having it and told Ms. Jensen to either be quiet or go back to her office and wait for security to escort her off the premises. That seemed to get her attention—she sat down and sulked for the remainder of the meeting.

When the meeting concluded, the board's chairman apologized to Baleigh for Ms. Jensen's behavior. He assured her they would be implementing her recommendations and hinted that she may be working with a different team when she returned in a few months. After speaking with him, she felt an urgent need to gather her things and get back to her hotel. She felt if she had to share any more space with Ms. Sally Jensen, she might very well tell her just how awful she was. Knowing her boss would frown upon that type of behavior she put her laptop and folders in her tote, grabbed her coat, and headed to the elevator as quickly as she could without being too obvious. Once the elevator doors closed, she reached into her tote for her phone and ordered an Uber.

Thankfully, a car was nearby, so her wait was short. She was ready to decompress. Once inside and on her way, she sat back and scrolled through her emails, thinking about the meeting she'd just left. The more she thought about that awful woman, the more she could feel her anger returning. She put her phone back in her bag and looked out of the window at the passing scenery. She'd been in this scenario before: go on a work assignment, get a ride back to the hotel, fly out the next day, go home, change clothes, repeat. Work was pretty much all she seemed to do. Her best friend Lisa said she spent too much time alone and had called her a workaholic on numerous occasions. Baleigh was starting to feel as if that might be true. She sighed deeply, and her vision blurred as her eyes started to water. *This is not good at all*, she thought. She needed to do better—make some changes.

After opening the door to her hotel room, her primary thoughts were taking off her shoes and having a glass of wine. She thought about having something stronger but decided against it. She was already feeling emotional and anything stronger would have her sad and fighting not to cry, the effects of which she knew she wouldn't want to deal with. She grabbed a wine glass and the bottle of pinot noir she'd purchased the day before and made her way over to the couch where she sat down, closed her eyes, and absorbed the quiet. The stillness was what she needed to get back to a sense of calm, but it was not to be, as her phone started to ring. She thought about ignoring it, but it was her work phone. Sighing because her tote was across the room, she begrudgingly got up, grabbed her phone from her tote, and answered.

"Hello, this is Baleigh."

"Hi, Baleigh, it's Celia. How's everything going?"

"Pretty good. This trip has been a bit trying, but we finished on a good note. How are things with you?"

"All is well. I can't complain."

"Nice. So, what's up? Not that I'm not happy to hear from you, but I usually don't hear from you during a trip unless it's urgent."

"Well, this isn't an urgent matter, per se. It's more of a request."

"A request?"

"Yes. A request. Simpson has a pressing family matter that's come up and needs someone to cover for him. Mr. Giles wanted me to give you a call to see if you could do it."

"Someone needs to do a check on Simpson. Seems like he is always having a pressing family matter. What is it this time? His wife wanted to celebrate buying a new bed for one of their children? Or was it the first time they planted flowers in their garden?" Baleigh said with more than a touch of sarcasm in her voice.

Celia laughed. "I have no idea," she said. "What I do know is that he made sure to close the door when he went in to speak with

Mr. Giles, so I wouldn't be able to hear him. When he left, he looked at me and did that smirk thing he does. Mr. Giles asked me to contact you. He wants to ask you himself, sort of as a personal favor. I'll put you through to him now."

"Thanks for the heads up, Celia. I appreciate it." In addition to being the executive assistant to Jefferson Giles, one of the owners of Giles and Associates, Celia was also a friend. While they weren't close, the two women looked out for one another and hung out together now and then.

"You're welcome, Baleigh." With that, Celia transferred the call.

"Hi, Baleigh, I just got off the phone with Todd Anderson, Baytown Healthcare's board chairman. He was singing your praises. Sally Jensen can be very difficult to deal with, and the board was impressed with how you handled the situation."

"Thanks, Jeff. While I appreciate the kind words, I have to say I'm surprised to hear from you."

"Yes, well, I'm sure you are. I'm calling to ask a favor. Simpson was assigned the Jarvis Health account, and he has a family emergency. This is an important account, and I need someone I can trust to handle it."

"I'm familiar with Jarvis Health, and I appreciate that you trust me enough to take care of it, but I've been on this assignment for two weeks and was looking forward to getting home and getting some downtime."

"I know you have. I also know that this wasn't an easy assignment. But, as you know, because of the complexities involved, I can't just reassign it to anyone. While I'm not above guilting you into accepting, I am asking you to take it as a personal favor to me."

Baleigh thought over his words. She'd been with Giles and Associates for five years and on Jeff's team for three. He was a good boss and mentor. As much as she wanted to say no, she knew she wouldn't. He rarely, if ever, made requests like this. "Oh, alright. But let me say two things about this. One, no matter how you frame it, this is a guilt trip. And two, I'd like to request a month off from travel when this assignment is done."

Jeff laughed. "You got me on that one. Thanks, Baleigh. I appreciate you taking this on. And your request is granted." Jeff gave her a few specific details about the client and told her he would personally email her the client information packet. He thanked her again before transferring her back to Celia to discuss her travel arrangements.

"So, what will it be? Since tomorrow is Thursday, do you want to go home as planned, then fly out on Sunday? I can also get you an early flight on Monday as well since your meeting with Mr. Jarvis is scheduled for eleven o'clock."

Baleigh listened to her options. While she wanted to go home and spend time in a familiar space, she knew she wouldn't get a chance to enjoy it since she'd have to turn around and fly right back out.

"You know what, Celia? I think I'll stay here and fly out Monday morning."

She waited as Celia checked flight schedules. "No flights going out early enough on Monday, but there's a red eye that leaves at 11:30 P.M. Sunday."

"That'll work. I'll call the front desk and extend my reservation."

"I'll finish booking your travel arrangements and send you the itinerary when I'm done."

"Thanks, Celia."

"You're welcome. Safe travels, and I'll see you in a few weeks. We'll do happy hour when you get back. First drinks are on me."

"Cool. See you then." Baleigh smiled as she ended the call. She'd been wanting to see some of the sights around town but hadn't gotten the chance because the client took up more time than anticipated. She'd been in River City, Oregon for the past two weeks. Spending some downtime here instead of going home for a day before getting back on the road would allow her to unwind a bit.

Pouring another glass of wine, Baleigh pondered her next steps since she'd be there for a few days. In addition to playing tourist, she needed to get her clothes to the hotel laundry and go over the client packet to prepare for Monday's meeting. First off, she contacted the front desk. With that done, she grabbed her suitcase, took out the clothes that needed to be laundered, and put them in the hotel's laundry bag. Next, she browsed through the hotel's brochures for local attractions. As she looked at the photographs, she felt the tears returning. The earlier feeling of sadness was starting to come back. Maybe these few days of downtime would help erase the blues she was experiencing. She hoped so. Her phone dinged, and she saw the email from her boss along with her travel itinerary. Placing her wine on the room desk, she reached for her laptop, opened it up, and started prepping for her next assignment.

Chapter 2

Morning arrived and with it, a strong desire to get the day started. After getting showered and dressed, she took a long look at herself in the mirror. At five feet seven inches, she was a few inches above average height. Her skin was the color of creamy peanut butter, and though she was in her late forties, her face bore little evidence of that fact. She wore her hair in a chin-length bob that flattered her face nicely. It was dyed a rich, chocolate-brown shade with subtle highlights, courtesy of an amazing hairstylist with whom she had a standing bi-weekly appointment. The color complemented her warm skin tone and her cognac-colored eyes. Since it was early fall, she dressed in layers, as the days began a little cold; they warmed up as the day went on. She had on a pair of jeans, a long-sleeved, soft gray and white striped t-shirt, topped with a dark blue V-neck sweater. She finished the look with tan suede ankle boots, and gold hoop earrings.

Baleigh was a woman with a woman's body. Her curves were not subtle in any form or fashion, and her jeans hugged her nicely. They were her favorite pair, and she never left home without them. They were like her little slice of home she carried with her wherever she went. The sweater she wore skimmed her waist and draped over the small pudge of her stomach. While many women her age were getting Botox or nips and tucks here and there to slow down the aging process, Baleigh was enjoying her body's transformation and worked to maintain good health and fitness. She applied light makeup, using powder, bronzer, mascara, and a clear gloss on her lips. Turning once more to get one last look, she was pleased with what she saw. She picked up her jacket, card key, purse and left her room, ready for the day ahead. She made a mental note to reschedule her next hair appointment as she headed to the elevator, where she ran into a hotel employee. On impulse, she asked him where she might get a good breakfast.

"Are you looking for anything specific?" he asked.

"No, just good food."

"There are a few places down the street from here that aren't half bad. If you don't mind walking, there's a pretty good diner. It's retro, and I like to go there whenever I get a chance. They have a typical breakfast menu and usually have specials."

"How far is it?"

"About six blocks."

"That's not bad. Which way is it?"

"When you exit the lobby, turn left, and walk six blocks. You'll see it as you approach."

She thanked him as they reached the lobby. Walking past the concierge's desk, she stopped to grab a few more of the brochures and stepped out into the brisk morning air. As she made her way to the diner, she felt the warmth of the sun despite the chill. This day was definitely off to a good start.

It didn't take her long to walk the six blocks. During the short walk, she thought about the decision she made to prolong her stay in the city. She really should have gone home to check on her place. She needed to do some laundry and run a few errands. After all, home was just a quiet place where she ate, slept, and changed clothes. She didn't have anyone or anything waiting for her, not even a plant. This was a spur-of-the-moment decision, something she rarely did, taking a day just for herself. She might as well take advantage of this unexpected opportunity. She didn't know when she'd get the chance to do so again.

Approaching the door of the diner, Baleigh saw it was busy. She gave her name to the hostess, Susan, according to the name tag, and waited to be seated. She took a moment to look around the diner. When the hotel guy told her it was retro, she thought he meant one of the typical 1950s type diners, which were common, but it felt like she was in a time warp. The place had more of a '70s feel and reminded her of the old-school diners she'd seen on television police dramas and movies from that era. Sooner than expected, the hostess came back and asked if Baleigh would mind sitting at the counter since it might be a bit longer than expected for her to get a table. Baleigh chose the counter and followed the hostess. After she sat down, the hostess set out a menu, silverware, and a glass of water.

"Would you care for coffee?" Susan asked. "We also have tea, juice, or fountain drinks if you prefer"

"Coffee will be fine."

Susan turned and spoke in another language to a man who was standing at the other end of the counter. Turning back, she smiled at Baleigh.

"Your server will be here shortly with your coffee."

"Thank you," Baleigh replied, and opened the menu.

As she was reviewing the menu, she noticed a man at the other end of the counter. He was dark-haired, of medium height, handsome, and muscular. He greeted her with a warm smile as he walked toward her and placed a cup next to her right hand, winking as he poured the coffee. Baleigh looked at him as she lifted the cup and took a sip and was pleasantly surprised at how good it was. Her facial expression showed such pleasure, he laughed at her surprise.

"Better than you were expecting?" he asked.

Baleigh smiled. "Yes, way better."

The man returned her smile. "We get that a lot."

He went on to give her the breakfast specials and told her he would be back to take her order when she was ready.

As he turned away, the man on the stool to her right called out to him.

"Nick, I need a refill and a twenty-letter word or phrase that is a play by Winston Smith. It starts with a "T" and ends with an "S.""

Nick, paused for a minute, thinking about a possible answer, then shrugged his shoulders, "I got nothing."

"This is the last clue for this puzzle. I can't figure it out."

The two men continued to go back and forth over possible answers to the clue as Nick refilled his cup.

Baleigh sat silently, drinking her coffee, observing the exchange. From the tone of their conversation, they seemed to be friends. They appeared to be somewhere between their mid-to-late forties, and both were handsome. Nick, the server, had salt-and-pepper colored hair and brown eyes to go with the muscular, stocky build she observed earlier. She couldn't see much of the man to her right other than his profile. He had dark, brownish-black hair that had silver threaded throughout, a goatee, and a very tense vibe about him.

"What was the clue again?" Nick asked.

"It's twenty letters and is the title of a play by Winston Smith. It starts with "T" and ends with "S.""

As she listened to him repeat it, the answer, which was *The Whiskey Chronicles* popped into her mind. Both men turned to look at her. She must have spoken the answer out loud.

The man who had been working on the puzzle turned in her direction and looked at her as if just noticing she was there.

"Excuse me?" he asked.

Baleigh looked at both men before responding, "The Whiskey Chronicles?"

He looked back at the puzzle as if mentally checking the answer, before writing it in the puzzle squares.

"Are you sure?"

"Yes."

He wrote the letters in their respective boxes.

"Yes, that's it." He put down his pen and turned to Baleigh. "Thank you."

Baleigh stared back and murmured something that sounded like, "You're welcome," and quickly turned her attention back to the menu. Looking at the man next to her had left her a little flustered. She didn't trust herself to not blurt out any of the thoughts that seemingly out of nowhere entered her head after he'd turned his full gaze upon her. At first glance of his profile Baleigh thought he might be handsome. Looking at him directly, she saw that she was right. What she had not expected was the way she felt when he looked at her. He was *very* handsome but not in a drop-dead gorgeous kind of way. He was white, but his skin was lightly tanned, as though he spent time outdoors. He had a chiseled jawline and a nose that had a slight bump along the ridge as if it had once been broken. His goatee was neatly trimmed, and like his hair, it too had silver strands. His eyes were hazel surrounded by thick, dark lashes that made his gaze a little more compelling than they were at first glance. His eyes also held a bit of something else that she couldn't discern.

Nick looked at the man and then at Baleigh. "Are you ready to order?"

"Yes. I'll have the Mediterranean omelet and Belgian waffle combo with a side of bacon."

"Good choice," he said. "Coming right up." As he walked towards the kitchen, he looked at the man once more and asked him if he had any more puzzle issues.

"No."

"Too bad," Nick smirked and continued his way to the kitchen.

Baleigh decided this would be a good time to look at the brochures she had brought with her. As she looked over the first one, she got the feeling she was being watched. She looked over at the man next to her. Sure enough, he was staring at her.

"On vacation?" he asked, glancing at the brochures she had placed on the counter.

"No," she replied. "I'm in town on business and have a free day, so I decided to check out the area. I got these from my hotel."

"Are you considering any place in particular?" He gazed directly at her as he spoke.

"I'm thinking about checking out the art museum, then maybe go over to the river walk."

He seemed to think about her answer for a minute and said, "Good choices. You'll like the museum."

She couldn't think of anything to say to that, so she looked back down at the brochure in her hand.

"Here you go," Nick said a few minutes later as he placed her order in front of her. The food looked and smelled delicious. Baleigh hadn't eaten since lunch the day before, so she was more than ready for breakfast. She picked up her fork and dug in with gusto. *This is good*, she thought as she tasted the omelet. It was made with egg whites and was light and fluffy. The vegetables tasted as though they were freshly picked from a garden behind the diner. She was enjoying each bite. Once again, feeling as if she were being watched, she looked over and saw Nick and the man looking at her. Nick had a grin on his face. The other had a frown. Nick began to laugh. "It's always a pleasure to see a woman enjoy her food. Would you care for more coffee?" Baleigh, feeling her face become a little warm, nodded.

Nick refilled her coffee cup and looked over at the brochures she'd placed on the counter. He asked Baleigh if she planned on doing some sightseeing. She answered as she had before, that she was planning to visit the art museum and then the river walk since they were both within walking distance. She also asked him if he could give her directions to the museum. Nick said he could. He then looked over at the man next to her.

"Sam, aren't you headed over to the museum today?" *Sam. So, that was his name,* Baleigh thought.

"Yes," Sam answered as he looked up from the paper he was reading.

"Why don't you be a good citizen and take Ms….?" He looked at her.

"Baleigh. Baleigh Emerson," she supplied.

"Why don't you take Ms. Emerson with you?"

Sam looked at Nick with narrowed eyes. Nick, smiling, looked back at Sam.

Baleigh quickly replied, "That's not necessary. I think I can find it okay."

Nick looked at her and said, "No, he'll do it. It's the least he can do since you helped him with that puzzle."

"I don't mind," Sam interjected. "I'm headed there anyway."

"In that case, uh, thanks," Baleigh said.

"And now that we've settled that, please allow me to make introductions. I'm Nick, and this is my friend, Sam. Sam McKinney."

"Nice to meet you both." She went back to eating her breakfast as the men continued to talk in-between Nick taking orders and refilling coffee. When she finished eating, she asked Nick for the check before she headed to the restroom.

Both men watched as she walked towards the ladies' room.

"What are you doing, Nick?" Sam asked.

"Nothing," he responded, hunching his shoulders.

"Are you really going to make me ask you again?"

Nick shrugged. "Lighten up. You've been moping around for months since you and Angela broke up. It won't kill you to have some fun for a change."

"How is this fun?" Sam asked.

"You're both going to the same place. You can be nice and show her around."

Sam started to say something else, but Baleigh returned. He decided to let it go, but not before giving Nick one last glare to let him know that the conversation was not over. Nick looked back at him. His smirk turned into a grin.

As Baleigh put on her jacket, she repeated her request for her check. Nick said since this was her first time here, and she helped his friend with his crossword puzzle, breakfast was on the house. Baleigh protested, but Nick insisted that he would not accept her money. Baleigh thanked him and left a generous tip, after all, the food and the unexpected conversation had been good. *Yes*, she thought again, *it looks as if it was going to be a good day.*

She looked over at Sam who was gathering his things. He shoved them into his messenger bag that hung on the back of his stool. He walked over toward the end of the counter and grabbed his jacket from the coat tree. She watched him walk and could not help but notice his body and how well his clothes fit. The dark green three-quarter zip sweater hugged his chest and shoulders. His jeans loosely fitted what looked to be a firm ass and hinted at some rather solid-looking thighs. His brown boots looked rugged and well-worn. *Well*, Baleigh thought to herself, *I could do a lot worse than going to the museum with Sam. Yes*, she thought, *looks like it's going to be a good day indeed.* She turned to Nick to say goodbye, and got a surprise. Judging by his expression, he had seen her checking out his friend. She quickly thanked him again, said goodbye, and walked to the door. Nick shook his head and laughed to himself as he watched them exit the diner. Baleigh walked through the door that Sam held for her and waited as he came out. She followed his lead as he turned left and walked beside him.

Chapter 3

"The art museum is about four blocks up this way, are you okay to walk?"

"I am. Although, I was expecting it to be a little warmer out here."

"It normally is. However, this year the weather has been a bit unpredictable."

With each not really knowing what to say to the other, they walked in silence. Sam seemed deep in thought. Rather than engage him in conversation, she looked at the surrounding scenery. There were lots of shops and restaurants lining both sides of the street. There were also a few office buildings. It was a mix of old and modern without one dominating the other.

As they continued to walk, she looked over at Sam. "You know, if you had other plans, I really could find my way to the museum."

He looked back at her. "No, breakfast and the museum were pretty much all I had planned for the day. I don't mind the company," he finished with a smile.

He had a nice smile. Surprised, Baleigh smiled back. "Okay, I'm glad we got that out of the way. Now, what can you tell me about this area? I've been here before, but I've never gotten around to taking in the lay of the land. From what I've read, this city has a rich and colorful history and lots of interesting characters."

Sam laughed. "That's true, and Nick is probably the most interesting character in that mix."

She laughed "I can see how that could be true."

They came to a corner and waited for the light to change. Sam drew her attention toward a small structure across the street. It looked like a toll booth of sorts that one might find on a bridge in a fairy tale. Baleigh was surprised to see it, as she had not noticed it before. He told her it was called "the love shack." As they got closer to it, she could see there were baskets attached to each side of the building. Sam told her that the artist who created the structure filled the baskets with what he called "love notes," each day. The artist was an aged hippie who believed that love was the missing element mankind needed, so he decided to use his notes to fill that void. *Well*, Baleigh thought, *he's not wrong. I could definitely use some love in my life.* She looked over at Sam as he continued to tell her about the artist and thought, *I wish.* As they came up to the building, Sam asked her if she wanted some love.

"Excuse me, what?" Baleigh asked, sure she hadn't heard him correctly.

"Do you want some love?" he asked, pointing to the baskets. "A love note," Sam said.

"Oh, no. It's still kind of early, and they probably haven't filled the baskets yet."

"Not a problem," Sam replied. "Chase would be happy to give you one if you wanted it. He's here pretty early most days. He and his wife fill the baskets themselves. Ah! Here he is now."

As if Sam had summoned him by talking about him, Chase Drummond, the artist, appeared from the other side of the building. He was a hippie/artist just as Sam had described him, and he'd aged well. He had thick, shoulder-length hair that was mostly white and looked as if it had once been blonde. He was wearing an embroidered cotton shirt and faded jeans. On his wrist were several leather and gold bracelets. He had a leather cord around his neck with a gold peace emblem hanging from it. His eyes were an unusual shade of blue, but what stood out most about him was the strong smell of marijuana that surrounded him. Yep, he smelled like weed. He approached them holding a basket in one hand and a joint in the other.

He greeted Sam with a hug and a smile. "How ya' doing, Sammy?" As he spoke to Sam, he looked over at Baleigh. "Who's your friend?"

"Baleigh, this is Chase, the artist who created this. Chase, Baleigh."

"Hi, Baleigh." Chase handed the basket to Sam and shook her hand. Sam glared at him as he took it. Chase then offered the joint to Baleigh, who smiled and shook her head in refusal. He put it between his lips and reached into the basket with his other hand, grabbed a folded note, and handed it to her.

"Here's a little souvenir from our love shack." He smiled and looked into her eyes as he gave it to her. His eyes were a beautiful turquoise blue and seemed to be staring right into her soul. It was as if he glanced into her mind and saw every secret she'd hidden there. Chase looked at Sam and said something. She couldn't hear what he said, but Sam didn't seem to like what he was hearing. Sam huffed and grabbed Baleigh's elbow just as she was about to read the note, and turned her back toward the sidewalk in the direction they'd originally been headed. Chase started to laugh and called out, "Goodbye!" Baleigh shoved the unread note into her pocket and turned to wave as Sam pulled her away.

Sam knew he was being rude when he abruptly ended his conversation with Chase. But at that moment, he didn't care. He considered the artist a friend, but every now and then, he found himself wondering why. Today was one of those days. What set

Sam off this time were five little words. "Angela is not coming back." That was it. Chase thought he was being helpful by reminding Sam that his former girlfriend of five years was gone, and there probably wasn't going to be a reconciliation as there had been in the past. Those five words made Sam catch his breath. It had been nine months since they broke up. He knew she wasn't coming back. He just hadn't been able to accept that fact and move on. Chase's words were a stark reminder of his inability to do so. Sam knew his friend had spoken those words out of love and not malicious intent; however, they still hurt to hear.

Baleigh felt a little confused as she quickened her steps to keep up with Sam. She found herself bothered by Sam's touch. She felt slightly off-kilter. This was the first time in a long time she'd been touched by a man who was not a friend, family member, or colleague. She wasn't expecting the slight tingle she felt when he touched her. She wasn't quite sure how to process it. To cover her unease, she concentrated on keeping up with Sam, who hadn't let go of her, nor had he slowed his pace. He didn't seem to be aware that she was rushing to keep up with him. She was tempted to slow down and see if he'd even notice. She was also starting to wonder why she ever agreed to go with him. Looked like the day was taking a turn. Maybe her earlier assessment had been wrong.

Chapter 4

Sam and Baleigh arrived at the museum. He took her coat and handed her a flyer with the current exhibit list. She looked it over while he made his way across the entrance to check their coats. He was still silent after the brief encounter with Chase, and she wasn't sure if she wanted to view the museum with him if he kept it up. There was a noticeably large distance between the two of them as they headed toward the first exhibit, which was a collection of oil paintings by a European master. They didn't speak as they viewed the paintings and Sam's body language made it evident he didn't want to engage in conversation.

The silence continued as they entered the next exhibit, which was a black and white photographic essay on the 1967 riots in Detroit, Michigan. Baleigh had heard about the exhibit and was looking forward to seeing it. As they stood in front of the placard with the photographer's bio, a pretty, tall, blonde woman walked over. She wore a blue skirt suit with a white shirt, and her name tag identified her as a museum docent.

"Sam! What a surprise! I was expecting to see you at the premiere last weekend," she exclaimed, her voice going a little breathless as she spoke. She spared a glance at Baleigh and quickly returned her full attention to Sam.

"Hi, Astrid. I wasn't able to make it," Sam said gruffly. He'd specifically chosen this time to visit because he remembered her telling him she didn't work mornings. She'd been hitting on him since they first met. He wasn't interested and had politely declined her invitations. She took his rebuffs as a 'maybe next time' and proceeded to plead her case whenever she got near him. He could have done without seeing her today. In addition to not being able to take a hint, she was also not very bright. Two things that did not work in her favor.

"Well, I'm glad you came today. I'd be happy to give you a tour." She placed her hand on his arm and smiled. "I'm only here for half a day today. Maybe, after the tour, we can grab some lunch."

Baleigh looked at the woman, then at Sam. She was curious to hear what his response would be, especially since he hadn't been too keen on going to the museum with *her* in the first place.

Sam looked down at Astrid's hand on his arm before replying, "I appreciate the offer, but I'll have to take a rain check. I'm showing my friend around."

"Your friend?" Astrid looked as surprised as she claimed to be earlier.

"Yes. Baleigh, this is Astrid. She's a docent here. Astrid, this is Baleigh. She's in town on business and I offered to show her the Jackson Thomas exhibit."

"In that case, I guess I'll catch up with you later." She pouted, reached up, kissed Sam on the cheek, and walked towards another section of the exhibit.

Baleigh looked at Sam. He returned her stare. "What?" he asked.

"What was that about?"

"Nothing."

She raised her eyebrows in question. "Nothing?"

"Nothing. I just didn't want her to show me around. I met her a few months ago when some of my work was part of an exhibit here. And I've run into her a few times since then."

"Wait," she said, forgetting about Astrid. "You're an artist?" *It would explain his moodiness,* she thought.

"A photojournalist, actually. This exhibit was done by one of my mentors."

"You knew Jackson Thomas?"

"I did. He was a friend of my father's. He introduced me to photography. I wanted to see this exhibit before it got crowded. It's very popular."

"I've heard about this exhibit. I'm glad I finally have a chance to see it."

"I guess we should get started." With that, he turned and led the way to the first set of photographs.

To say that she was surprised to learn Sam was a photojournalist was an understatement. However, she was impressed when she learned he'd been mentored by Jackson Thomas, an African American Pulitzer Prize-winning photographer whose pictorial essay of America during the 1950s-1970s was housed in the Smithsonian Museum. Sam, it seems, kept good company. They quietly began to talk as they slowly viewed the exhibit. The stark, emotional destruction displayed in the photographs was so palpable, it was as if one could hear the angry voices and the wail of the sirens if one listened closely enough. The tears, sadness, anger, and fear were all on display. As they walked side-by-side, it was as if they absorbed the authenticity of the moments; they were seeing a sort of tension begin to escalate between them. The realness of the pictures unexpectedly brought up unwanted memories for each of them. For her, her failed marriage, and her unhappiness with her job and her life. For him, memories from one of his many times in war zones, all of which he would much rather forget. Somehow, their discussion became less about the photographs and more about their feelings. Baleigh could tell by his short answers that Sam was getting either angry or annoyed. She felt sadness mixed with anger and a sense of loss, and by the time they'd gotten halfway through the exhibit, they were both silent again, absorbed by their own personal thoughts. A stranger walking by would be hard-pressed to believe the two of them were together.

At this point, Sam had no desire to see the rest of the exhibit. Yes, he'd committed himself to spend part of the day with Baleigh, but what he wanted to do was take her back to her hotel and go find the nearest bar. Baleigh looked close to tears. As much as he wanted this museum excursion to be over, he realized he couldn't just cut it short. He needed to try and salvage the day. After all, he'd agreed to show her around. He needed to get out of his feelings. As quickly as things had gone south, he could at least try to get them back on an even keel.

Baleigh was struggling with the onslaught of unexpected feelings. Her plan for the day had been to do a little sightseeing and some soul searching, not stand in the middle of an art museum on the verge of a meltdown. She also hadn't anticipated being accompanied by a handsome man whose brooding cast a cloud over everything in his path. She needed to get herself together. She mentally calculated the distance to her hotel. Maybe she should leave. Since she was going to be there for a few more days, she could always come back and see the rest of the exhibits another time. As Baleigh mulled over an exit strategy, Sam interrupted her thoughts.

"I, um, have a studio near here."

She looked questioningly at him.

"If you're interested, we can go. I can show you some of my work."

"I don't know…" she began.

"Look, I know this has been awkward. And I know it's mostly my fault. I don't know what else you had planned for the day, but I'd like to make it up to you."

Looking into his eyes, she saw sincerity. Perhaps he was sorry for his behavior. However, she wasn't quite willing to give him a second chance to possibly screw up more of her day. Her skepticism must have been reflected on her face.

"Seriously, Baleigh. I think you might enjoy seeing the studio."

"Okay, I'll go. But I'm not quite over being pissed with you just yet."

"Great." Sam smiled. "Let's go. My studio is a few miles from here. We can grab an Uber out front."

This was the second time today she found herself caught up in the unexpected appearance of his smile. It transformed the gruff demeanor of what she'd begun to assume was his normal brooding countenance to handsome. As few and far between as his smiles seemed to be, when they appeared, they were genuine and were reflected in his hazel eyes, which seemed to change with his mood.

"Um, sure. But I want to stop by the restroom before we go."

"There's one near the exit." he touched her arm to guide her in that direction. Walking beside her, he tried to ignore the warm spark he felt when Baleigh accepted his offer.

When they reached the exit, Sam got their jackets while Baleigh went to the ladies' room. As she stood in front of the mirror washing her hands, she gave herself a mental pep talk. She'd told him she'd go with him to his studio, but she wasn't sure it was a good idea. He hadn't exactly said the words, but the invitation he'd extended was an apology. Maybe she should tell him she'd changed her mind, and go back to her hotel instead. He probably wouldn't care. He would probably be relieved. *Yeah*, she thought. *I'm just going to tell him I changed my mind.* Once that was settled, Baleigh continued her inner dialogue as she placed her hands under the automatic air dryer. *When he hands me my coat, that's when I'll tell him.*

Despite her intention to do otherwise, five minutes later, Baleigh found herself sitting in the back seat of an Uber with Sam, headed to his studio. Disappointed that she wasn't able to stick with her decision, she decided that rather than tempt fate and give him a reason to revisit his previous funky mood, she'd just sit quietly and enjoy the ride. She'd speak if he engaged *her* in conversation, but that was it. Once they arrived, she planned to view his work and head back to her hotel as quickly as she could.

After numerous attempts to talk with Baleigh during the ride to his studio, Sam gave up. Her answers were short, or she simply smiled, or looked out the window, as if wanting to avoid eye contact with him. *What the hell was that about?* She'd talked to him more when they were back at the museum. He assumed she'd forgiven him when she accepted his offer, but now he wasn't so sure. Maybe she was still upset. Maybe she was crazy. Who knew? Dealing with women's emotions was one of the reasons he hadn't moved on to another relationship. *That and your broken heart*, his conscious quickly reminded him. Sam sat beside Baleigh, wondering how he found himself in his current situation with a woman who might be emotionally unstable or emotionally unavailable. Or maybe she was just pissed. She was good to look at though, but then again, the crazy ones always are.

Perhaps picking up on the tension between Sam and Baleigh, the Uber driver turned on the radio and started to sing along. Sam scrolled through his phone and rudely asked him to stop singing. Baleigh's sharp intake of breath at his request showed her shock at his rudeness. She gave the driver an apologetic look and glared at Sam. Thankfully, they arrived at their destination and exited the car.

"I don't know what your problem is," Sam told her as they walked on the path that led to his studio. "If you hadn't been trying to ignore me, you would have realized the driver was a horrible singer." With that, he unlocked the door to the studio, opened it, and stepped back to allow her to enter. Baleigh tried hard to hide the small smile that appeared at his words. He was right. The driver really had been an awful singer.

Chapter 5

Although amused at his comment, Baleigh wasn't willing to give him a pass. She felt her anger rising again and proceeded to let him know exactly what she thought about his rudeness and pretty much everything else that she'd been feeling about him.

"You know, Sam, I don't know where you get off thinking you can say anything you want to anyone and seem to think it's okay when it's not."

"Come again?"

"You heard me. Your rude and obnoxious behavior. If I wanted to be in miserable company, I could have stayed at the hotel. Instead, I'm here with you."

"Look, Baleigh, I already apologized. What more do you want? I'm fresh out of ideas, so you're going to have to help me out because I don't know what else to do with you."

"What else to do with me? I don't need you to do *anything* with me. I was getting along fine before I met you this morning, and I'm sure I will continue to do so."

"Well, maybe you should act like it then. Maybe you should go back to your hotel. Or better yet, maybe you should just cut your trip short and go home. Clearly, you don't seem to be able to keep your emotions in check."

Baleigh's breathing quickened. His words reminded her of another argument that took place two months ago with Rod, her boyfriend of two years. They were similar to those uttered by Sam. *"You don't seem to be able to keep yourself together emotionally."* Rod had accused her of not being able to provide him with the type of encouragement and support he needed. His last words to her before walking out of her life were, "I think we're done here." Back in the present, the anger she felt increased as she felt tears well up in her eyes. Alarmed at the sight of Baleigh's warm brown eyes filling with tears, Sam quickly tried to console her. "Baleigh, are you okay? I'm sorry, I didn't mean to make you upset. I…" At his attempt to calm her, Baleigh burst into tears, horrified that she was losing control in front of Sam.

What was happening?! She was not a woman given to emotional displays. Somehow, his words about her emotions had touched a nerve. *It was true*, she thought. She had been struggling emotionally since she'd broken up with Rod. Her self-pity had also led her to isolate herself from her friends, family, and any potential relationships. As much of a jerk as Sam had been, he'd inadvertently called her on her actions, whereas others had simply avoided the whole thing and allowed her to wallow in her sadness. She turned away from him and tried to stem the flow of her tears.

Sam was at a loss as to what just happened. Whatever it was, he got a sense that it might not be so much about him. He placed his hand on her shoulder and felt her immediately try to move away from him. He gave her shoulder a gentle squeeze and suggested she have a seat. She gave a small nod, and he led her over to a chair near the window. He gave her a handkerchief and moved away from her. He returned shortly with a bottle of water, which he shoved into her hand before taking a seat across from her.

"Do you want to talk about it?" Sam asked.

Baleigh heard his question but didn't answer because she didn't know what to say. She wasn't sure what had just happened or why it was happening now. Perhaps she wasn't as good at handling her issues as she thought she was if she was triggered by what had just been a silly argument.

"Baleigh?"

"I don't want to talk about it." She sighed, not quite able to make eye contact with Sam. "Besides, if I did, I wouldn't know what to say."

"Based on your reaction just now, something is *definitely* wrong."

"And talking to you is going to help me figure out what it is?" Baleigh asked angrily. "Forgive me if I find that hard to believe."

Sam looked at Baleigh, trying to decide if he should continue this conversation that appeared to be going nowhere, or if he should just get her back to her hotel. He was about to suggest the latter, but his earlier words gave him pause. He'd said he wanted to make up for his behavior. He had every intention of doing so, but so far, he hadn't been successful. He needed to do better.

"Look, Baleigh," Sam took a deep breath, "you don't have to talk about it if it makes you uncomfortable. I know I haven't been the best of company today, and truth is, I'm not the best of company on most days. But it was never my intention to upset you. I was serious earlier when I said I wanted a do-over for the day. I still want that, but I understand if you want to go back to your hotel. I hope you don't, but if you do, I'll take you back."

Baleigh took in Sam's words as she tried to stop the flow of tears. Yes, he'd been an asshole, but this was more about her than it was about him. He wasn't the best of company, but he didn't seem the type to be deliberately hurtful. She took a drink from the water bottle he'd given her.

"I don't want to talk about it, Sam. I appreciate your offer to do so; however, this is something I need to deal with on my own." She paused a bit to gather her thoughts as to what she wanted to say next. "And you're right, you're not good company," she said with a weak smile. "But bad company or not, if the offer is still good, I'd like to see your work."

Sam chuckled at that. After giving her time to compose herself, he asked if she was ready to see the studio.

Viewing Sam's photographs, Baleigh was amazed at his talent. Most of the photographs were depictions of war-torn places and the resulting poverty and destruction. They were so vivid, that it felt as if she was experiencing them with each of her senses. What made this more remarkable was that the renditions displayed on television and the internet did not do them justice. Based on what she saw, she could only imagine what it must have been like for Sam in those places, taking those pictures. *Seems he might be dealing with some demons of his own*, she thought. When she got to the last picture, she stole a glance at his profile as he stood looking out of a nearby window. The anger she felt towards him earlier began to fade. As if sensing she was done, Sam turned away from the window and walked towards her.

"We've been viewing pictures for a while. I was thinking about grabbing a late lunch when you're done. Would you care to join me?"

Surprised, Baleigh hesitated before responding, then smiled. "You mean if I'm done crying."

"That too." Sam chuckled.

"Yes, I think I would." She was still feeling a little raw from her earlier mini-meltdown and from the pictures she'd viewed.

"There's a Brew Haus restaurant that has a pretty good menu as well as a nice sampling of some of the local beers. If you don't mind going, it's just a short walk along the river path from here."

"Sounds pretty good. I'm up for it."

"Let me lock up, and we can get going." Sam put the picture portfolios Baleigh had been viewing away, opened the door for her, then locked the studio. Using his cell phone, he set the alarm.

"This way." He pointed to a park across the street that ran along the river. They crossed over and began to follow along the path he'd mentioned earlier, making small talk as they walked along. The mood had changed. It was companionable, the underlying tension significantly lower than it had been earlier. It was beginning to morph back into an awareness of each other they both experienced earlier but tried to ignore.

After being seated, the host gave them menus and a list of beers they offered. Baleigh alternated between looking at her menu and glancing at Sam across the table from her. Between the time they left his studio and now, she'd gotten curious about him. Maybe he wasn't the brooding and slightly moody man she thought he was. Apparently, there was more to him than she originally thought. Too bad she wouldn't get a chance to find out, since she'd be heading back to her hotel after they finished their meal. Their server brought their drink orders and an awkward silence ensued. Although he appeared to be a little more relaxed than he had been all day, Sam still seemed a bit uncomfortable as he sipped his beer.

"Thanks again, Sam, for spending time with me today and showing me your studio."

"You're welcome."

"I enjoyed seeing your work. I'm still surprised that you knew Jackson Thomas. I can't imagine what it must have been like to get a chance to work with him."

"I'm still amazed that I was blessed with that opportunity. He had a gifted eye. He created phenomenal stories with his camera that brought the world to life in a way that made you feel that you were right there watching things unfold." Sam gave a small smile that reached his eyes.

"So, in addition to being his mentee, you were also a fan?" she asked.

"Guilty." He chuckled lightly. "As I mentioned earlier, he and my dad were friends. Once, when my mom was sick, my dad had to take her to the hospital. Mr. Jackson picked me up from school and let me hang out with him at his studio. I remember him showing me some of his cameras and the pictures he'd taken. After that one day, I was hooked."

"Nice." Taking a sip of her beer, Baleigh noticed a change in his eyes as he spoke about his mentor and friend. They took on a softness that spoke of the depth of feeling she was surprised to see. Sam was a man of many layers. She never would have guessed.

"So began my life-long journey into the world of photography and photojournalism," Sam said, picking up the conversation.

Their conversation paused as their server brought their food. They both ordered burgers, his with fries and hers with house-made potato chips. She popped a warm, lightly salted chip into her mouth.

"Mmmm," Baleigh said as she reached for a few more chips.

Sam watched her as she ate. Based on her reaction, they seemed to be pretty good.

"That good, huh?"

Slightly embarrassed, she nodded. "That good. Would you like to try a few?"

"I think I might." He looked at her as he spoke and watched as she moved her plate closer to him.

"Here, have some."

Sam reached across the table and took a few from the plate she offered. He ate one, then frowned as he looked at the remaining chips he'd taken. "They taste better than my fries. How does that happen? They're both fried potatoes with salt."

Baleigh laughed. "I don't know. I just know I like fresh-made chips with my burgers and sandwiches. How about we share? I'll give you half of my chips for half of your fries?"

"Normally, I would say no. But since these taste better than my fries, I'll take you up on your offer." He shoved his plate toward hers. She took half of the fries from his plate, and he did the same with the chips from hers.

"Now every time I come here, I'm gonna have to order chips instead of fries. I think you ruined them for me," he said as he placed another chip in his mouth, his expression changing when he saw her dip a fry in mayonnaise and eat it. "Mayo on your fries?"

"Best way to eat them. You should try it."

"I'll pass." He shook his head as he spoke.

The conversation came to a lull again as each ate their food. Baleigh wanted to apologize for her earlier outburst but wasn't ready to address it just yet. Maybe if she had another beer. After all, the man *had* changed his plans for the day and taken her around. Yes, he'd kinda been a jerk at times, but overall, he'd been nice. He deserved an apology.

While Baleigh was struggling with her internal thoughts, Sam was wrestling with a few of his own. Somewhere between the art museum and their arrival at the restaurant, he'd started to become fascinated by her. He was surprised she knew as much as she did about his mentor and his work. She'd gotten a little angry when they were at the museum, which was his fault, however, he hadn't expected the tears back at the studio. He probably should have taken her back to her hotel, but he found he didn't want to. He wanted to make sure she was okay, hence the offer to eat. Even though they hadn't talked much, he found himself enjoying her company and wanted to know more about her. *Maybe she was interested, too*, he thought. Almost like she read his mind, Sam was surprised when she asked him a question more personal than the others so far.

"You're pretty familiar with everything around here. Are you originally from here or are you a transplant from somewhere else?"

"I'm local. I grew up not too far from here. Nick and I grew up together."

"Nick?"

"From the diner this morning."

"The guy who got you stuck with me today?" Baleigh smiled.

"Yes, that guy. He, myself, and Jay, another friend, met at a group meeting when we were little. We attended the same schools from elementary to high school."

"What kind of group were you all part of?"

"Our fathers served in Vietnam. They'd been having some problems and were attending group therapy. One of the sessions was for families, and that's where we met. At first, our parents thought it was a good thing, but after all the stuff we got into over the years, I'm sure there were times they wished we'd never met." Sam laughed as he picked up his beer and took a drink.

More than a few sentences from Sam encouraged her to keep going. She could tell that he and Nick were probably good friends by the way they interacted back at the diner, along with their other friend. She wondered about some of the adventures they might have had. Having moved a lot while growing up and being an only child to a single parent who'd also been an only child, Baleigh didn't grow up with the childhood friendships that most people experience in their youth.

"What happened after high school?"

"We went in different directions. I went to a school here in the area. Jay went out of state, and Nick went to a culinary institute. We all ended up back here. Both Jay and I were in Nick's wedding a few years ago."

"Any siblings?"

"No. Just Nick and Jay who are pretty much my brothers in every way that counts. How about you? Any brothers and sisters?"

"No. Just me. I am an only child and so is my mother. It was just me and her, and we moved around a lot. We didn't put down roots until my junior year of high school. Like you, I stayed local for college and after. I met my best friend in college, and let's just say, she encouraged me to get out and stretch my boundaries."

They talked a little more about their growing-up years and friendships until their server came by and asked them if they needed anything else. Sam looked at Baleigh, who shook her head before answering "no" to the server and asking for the check. Sam glanced at the bill, removed his wallet, and placed a few bills on the table and stood up. Baleigh stood as well. She grabbed her jacket and purse and walked ahead of him out of the restaurant. Standing outside she decided now was the time to apologize, if she wanted to get it out before they parted ways.

"Thanks, Sam. I appreciate you taking me around today and for the meal."

"You already thanked me. And besides, I was hungry, and I figured you might be, too."

"I also wanted to apologize." She fiddled with her jacket as she spoke, avoiding his eyes.

"Apologize for what?"

"For having a meltdown in your studio. You'd already given up your day. You didn't need to be a witness to that, too."

"You don't have to apologize. I could have been a little nicer."

"You could've." She gave a sad smile. "But it wasn't your fault. I've been dealing with a lot lately, and somehow, today was the day things came to a head."

"How about we call it even? If you're not in a hurry to get back, the river walk goes past your hotel." Sam looked at her, waiting for her to answer the real question he was silently asking her. He told himself it was the least he could do to finish up the day on a good note, but the truth was, he wanted to spend a little more time with her. There was something about Baleigh that reached out to him and made him feel at ease. It might have been her sometimes awkwardness or the absence of predatory vibes he'd gotten from some of the dates he'd forced himself to go on. An unexpected desire, one he had not had in a long time had sprung up, surprising him. He'd been struggling in his attempts to move on from his last relationship.

As draining as the day had been, things didn't go as far south as they could have. Besides, she'd rather spend more time with Sam than indulge in a bottle of wine and a possible pity party.

"Sure. I'd like that."

He gave her one of his rare smiles. "Let's go."

Walking along the river path, Sam pointed out various buildings and statues and told her a little more about the history of the city. She was surprised to learn the colorful and slightly weird culture had pretty much been around since it had originally been founded. Baleigh found herself laughing out loud at some of the stories Sam recounted about the first settlers. They'd planned to set up a utopia but ended up with a town like most other towns in the early West, with what could be considered for that time, a new-age twist. In addition to townsfolk, ranchers, and cowboys, there were also astrologers, psychics, and other self-proclaimed mystics. Amazingly, they all seemed to get along. Over the years, the town grew and continued to maintain its original vibe.

Arriving at her hotel, Baleigh turned to face Sam. "I know you said no thanks needed, but I'm thanking you again anyway. I had a wonderful time."

He gave her a lopsided grin. "I'll accept the thanks if you promise no more meltdowns." That made her laugh.

Looking at each other, they both laughed. Baleigh stepped closer to Sam and hugged him. He clumsily reciprocated as if it had been a while since he'd done so. Encouraged by his response, she reached up and kissed him. Sam initially hesitated, then kissed her back. As she opened up to the kiss, she felt the softness of his lips and the feel of his body as he pulled her closer. She was surprised when he deepened the kiss, and the heat it generated in her body brought with it an unexpected longing. And just as quickly as it began, the kiss ended. He leaned his forehead against hers for a few seconds, then turned and walked away. Baleigh watched him as he left and thought about the kindness of strangers. When she hugged him, she'd put her card with her contact information in his pocket. She wondered if he would find it.

Chapter 6

After a hot shower and two glasses of wine later, there was a knock on her door. Baleigh looked through the peephole and saw Sam. She opened the door and they stood looking at each other for a long minute.

"You found the card," she said, motioning him inside.

"I did." He crossed the threshold and entered the room. He closed the door, grabbed her, turned her around, gently moved her back against it, and kissed her.

Baleigh didn't know what shocked her more; Sam in her room, Sam pressing his big body up against hers, or Sam kissing her. All three felt damn good. It had been a long time since she'd been kissed by a man. She'd been on a few dates here and there, but beyond a hug or a peck on the cheek, there wasn't much more physical interaction, and there definitely was none of the heat she was feeling now. This kiss was different from the one she and Sam had shared earlier. This kiss was hot, wet, and intense.

"I just wanted to spend a little more time with you," Sam said as he placed a kiss just below her ear. His warm breath, his lips upon her skin, and his nearness caused her to sigh as she allowed herself to feel the sensations that coursed through her body.

"I want that, too," Baleigh responded breathlessly.

Sam stepped back and looked at her, his hazel eyes appearing more green than brown, and full of desire. The intensity of his gaze gave her pause, and at that moment, she felt if he were of a mind, he could not only have his way with her body, but she could also allow her heart to open for him. She welcomed the former and wasn't sure if she'd be able to recover from the latter. She didn't know how she knew it, but she was certain it was true. She didn't care though. She needed this time with him. She needed to feel all the emotions he was stirring up inside of her. It had been too long, and until now, she hadn't wanted to give herself over to them. She did now, and she would.

Sam hadn't planned to see Baleigh again once they parted at her hotel. The hug and the kiss they'd shared had affected him. He hadn't anticipated that either, but once he felt her arms around his neck and breathed in the smell of her perfume, he found himself wanting more of her. When she kissed him, it felt so good, he had to kiss her back. He pulled her closer to get better access to her beautiful mouth and the havoc it was generating through him. He hadn't been ready for it. That's why he pulled back, said good night, and left. Trying to make sense of the turmoil he was experiencing, he decided against taking an Uber and walked the mile or so distance back to his home as he sorted through his thoughts. It was when he arrived home and reached into his pocket for his keys that he found Baleigh's card. He had no idea when she would have placed it there. He walked into the kitchen, took a glass from the cabinet, walked over to the refrigerator, and filled it with water. He leaned against the counter, where he placed the glass after draining it, and looked at the card again. Her email and cell number were neatly printed, and she'd handwritten her suite number at the hotel. Tapping the card against his other hand, he decided that he would pay her a visit. He didn't know what would happen once he arrived, but he planned to find out.

Now, here he was. When he knocked, he didn't know if she'd answer, much less let him in. When she opened the door, she was barefoot and wearing a tank top and matching boxer shorts. He knew she was curvy but seeing those curves displayed as they were now made his mouth water. Her surprise at his appearance was evident on her face as she stepped aside to let him enter. Wanting to feel the touch of her mouth upon his once more, he eased her back against the door and kissed her. The feel of her body against his as he leaned into her gave rise to a wanting of so much more. He didn't know if that would happen; he just knew he needed to be in the same space with her, and he told her so. When she responded in kind, he took her hand and led her over to the couch.

Baleigh was having a hard time paying attention, as she was reliving the kiss they'd just shared. She didn't realize just how much until Sam called her name. She shook her head slightly and asked him to repeat what he'd said. His eyes sparkled knowingly as if he understood the effect he was having on her.

"I asked if you would mind if I had a glass of wine."

"No, let me get you a glass." Her hands shook slightly as she retrieved his glass and lifted the bottle. She felt his eyes on her and hoped she didn't spill it. Thankfully, she was successful and handed it to him without mishap. His fingers lingered on hers for a short beat as he took the glass from her. He smirked as he raised it to his lips.

Sam could tell Baleigh was nervous. She tried to hide it but wasn't quite able to. He'd seen her display an array of emotions today, but the vulnerability she was revealing made her that much more beautiful to him. He wanted to put her at ease, but he also wanted to stoke a fire in her to match the one inside of him. He knew it was there. He'd felt its spark when they kissed.

He waited until she sat down on the couch and then he purposely sat close to her, partly because he wanted the connection and to see how she would react to his nearness. It was more of the latter. The few times they'd touched earlier, he'd felt a jolt of something. And the kiss—well, he couldn't stop thinking about it. He wanted to kiss her again to see what would happen.

He set his wine on the table in front of them, watching Baleigh as he leaned back against the cushions, and idly ran his hand over the exposed skin of her thigh, just below the edge of her shorts. He heard her breath catch and watched in fascination as she squeezed her legs together. *Yes*, he thought to himself, *she is just as affected as me*. He reached across and took the wine glass from her, setting it next to his. He took her hand and kissed her palm, then pulled her towards him, gently cupping the back of her neck. Her gaze cast shyly downward as he drew her closer. His hand moved from her neck to her cheek, and his thumb slowly slid across her lower lip. He tilted her head until her gaze met his. Her eyes reflected the desire he felt building. He leaned forward and touched his lips to hers. He immediately felt the spark reignite from when she unexpectedly kissed him earlier. A touch of lips became a hot, open-mouth kiss with tongues intertwined. The intensity of it grew as she wrapped her arms around his neck and moved closer. Without breaking their connection, Sam shifted their bodies so that she lay back against the cushions underneath him. His hands roamed over her body, touching her, and reveling in the satiny-soft feel of her skin. His lips moved to her neck and continued to travel downward.

Baleigh was kissing Sam and thoroughly enjoying it. He'd surprised her with his unexpected visit, and even more so when he pushed her up against the door. She was enjoying his kiss. Her whole body was. She could feel the wetness forming in her core, the warmth of his body, his touch, and his kiss. Who knew a few kisses from him would create such a reaction? Without breaking contact, he laid her back along the cushions and covered her with his body. She could feel his erection as his body shifted over hers. His hands seemed to be everywhere at once. She ran her hands up his torso and undid the buttons of his shirt, sliding her hands along the warm smoothness of his chest. His hands moved to the bottom of her tank top, pulled it off, and lowered his head to take a nipple into his mouth. He swirled his tongue around the areola of the one and massaged the other, pulling it between his thumb and forefinger. His touch was not gentle, but it didn't hurt either. Baleigh found herself sinking into the pleasure and pain of it. His other hand was in pursuit of something more as it made its way down to the waistband of her shorts. His lips returned to hers as his hand traveled further down, finally taking in the wetness that soaked her shorts. He ran his fingers through the slickness and began to rub her clit, creating delicious friction. He continued to play with both her nipples and clit as he kissed her. He was engaging her senses in a manner that connected them in a way she had not expected.

He broke the kiss, and Baleigh, feeling the loss of his lips, opened her eyes and found him gazing at her. Without him speaking, Baleigh knew what he was asking. But she was not quite able to answer verbally, so she gave him a nod of consent as he was still rubbing her clit, making her juices flow with each movement. Gently sucking her bottom lip, he delved deeper into her mouth, completely enveloping her in the act of their tongue play. Baleigh felt the pinch to her clit and her nipple at the same time, triggering an unexpected orgasm that caused her to break the kiss and scream her pleasure. Slowly, Sam removed his hand and smiled, looking her straight in the eye as he licked his fingers, taking in the taste of her.

"Are you okay?" he asked.

"Yes," she said on a sigh. Hearing the breathlessness of her voice reminded her that this was the first orgasm she'd had in two years that didn't come with a little help from her B.O.B. (battery operated boyfriend).

"Shall we continue?"

"God, yes!"

"Let's move to the bed. We're going to need the extra room." He gave her a sexy, lop-sided grin as he spoke.

When they made it to the other side of the room, she was sans her top but still had on her shorts and was feeling a little self-conscious about her body. Sam stood over her, tall and sexy, never taking his eyes off her as he finished removing his shirt and began to undo his pants. She wanted to look away and cover herself but found herself unable to do either.

Sam noticed that Baleigh seemed a little shy as she stood by the bed, removing her shorts as she watched him undress. He found it adorable. He held her gaze, almost daring her to look away. The way she came while they were on the couch had him getting even harder at the thought of how good she would feel coming on his cock. He knew from their first kiss there was more to her than the tense, slightly sad vibe she gave off. Her passion had been hiding just below the surface. The kisses gave a glimpse, but the way she tasted had him wanting more. Rock hard with his boxer briefs still on, he stood next to the bed and watched as she climbed on and crawled to its center. He placed a condom next to the pillow, tossing a few more on the nightstand before he removed his underwear, immediately covering her body with his own.

Baleigh felt the skin-to-skin contact as he kissed her. His work-worn hands were incredibly gentle as they roamed her body. He raised himself up and smoothed her hair away from her face and just stared, almost like he was taking in her features to later remind him of this moment. He saw the raw desire in her eyes, and he was sure his reflected the same. He leaned down and kissed her once more, this time with rising passion. His hand reached down, and he slowly began to stroke her pearl, then increased the tempo and friction before inserting a finger into her core where he was met with hot, wet, tightness. He added another finger, increasing the speed, listening to Baleigh's moans of pleasure, and feeling her body respond to him. He turned his palm upward and curled his fingers in a soft, back-and-forth motion, keeping the same momentum, and was rewarded as the walls of her pussy clenched his fingers and her body began to buck. He held her in place and placed his mouth over hers to devour her cries as her second orgasm shot through her.

Wasting no time, he grabbed the condom, and quickly sheathed himself, and positioned his cock at her entrance. He looked at Baleigh, who shyly looked away as she tried to calm her breathing. Sam cupped her cheek and guided her gaze back to him. He rubbed the tip of his cock against her lower lips, smearing her wetness. With each teasing stroke, he felt her body rise to meet his, only to be denied what she wanted. Her breathing, her scent, and the sound of her voice as she whimpered and moaned caused him to abandon the teasing play and enter her completely in one quick stroke. He'd felt her heat and wetness, but the way her body fit his; well, he hadn't been prepared for that. The slick tightness of her pussy was of another level.

"Damn, Baleigh," was all he could say as he felt her body begin to tremble with the onset of another orgasm. Sam continued to thrust into her body, reveling in the vibrating and clenching around his cock. He increased his rhythm and played with her clit as he coaxed her to come again, this time joining her. He watched as she closed her eyes and listened as she gave herself over to the pleasure of her release. The pulsing connection of their bodies was so intense, that he found himself struggling to catch his breath.

Baleigh slowly opened her eyes and found herself staring into Sam's warm gaze. Both were breathing heavily; both were covered with sweat and smiling. Not quite having the words to express what she wanted to say, she reached up and kissed him, hoping to convey them through her actions. When their heartbeats slowed and their breathing returned to normal, Sam got up and went to the bathroom and disposed of the condom. He returned with a warm, wet cloth.

His touch was gentle. It felt like a continuation of their previous lovemaking and made her feel special and cared for. Afterward, as they lay next to each other, Sam held her in a way that made her feel sublime. Baleigh knew with certainty what he was giving her at that moment was something she'd never experienced before but hoped to again.

"How much longer will you be in town?"

"I'll be here for two more days."

"I can show you more of the sites if you're interested."

Baleigh looked at him for a long moment before answering, "I am."

"Okay."

She rose up and eyed him. "Okay," she said, echoing him. She leaned forward, and he met her halfway. When they came together, Sam shifted her body so that she lay on top of him.

"Okay," he repeated and smiled as he reached over to the nightstand where he'd tossed the other condoms earlier. Baleigh gently removed it from his hand, smiling as she looked down at Sam. Tearing the wrapper open, she couldn't think of any place she'd rather be at that moment than engaging in round two with him.

When morning came, she was expecting awkwardness or the weirdness that came with the morning after a one-night stand. What she felt instead was satisfaction, a little soreness, and warmth from the man who was spooning her. She wondered if he was planning to follow through with his offer to show her around. Just in case he reneged, she decided to savor the moment. While she was taking it all in, she felt him move. Then she heard him say good morning. She shivered as she felt his breath against the back of her neck as he spoke.

"I know I asked you this last night, but when will you be heading back home again?"

"I'm leaving out Sunday night. I'm not going home though. I picked up a new assignment, so I'll be going to L.A. instead."

"Still interested in seeing the area?"

"Is the offer still good?" she asked, turning around to look at him.

"It is."

"Then I'm still interested." She smiled.

"If you want, you can get ready now and come back with me to my place so I can change, or I can go and come back to get you."

"I'll get ready now. No need for you to make an extra trip."

While she was in the shower, Sam had gone out and grabbed coffee and scones. She thought it was sweet of him to do so as she sipped on her coffee and finished getting ready. She wore a long sleeve black dress that fit smoothly over her curves and stopped mid-calf. She draped a colorful scarf around her neck and slipped on a pair of comfortable black flats. She added a pair of gold earrings and a berry-tinted lip gloss. Done, she walked from the dressing area back into the room where she found him munching on a scone and reading the newspaper provided by the hotel. He looked up from the paper and smiled as she walked toward him. He grabbed the bag with the scones he held it out to her. Reaching inside, she grabbed one, sat down next to him, and ate it while he continued to read the paper. When he was done, he took a page from the paper, folded it, and put it on the table. She could see that it was a crossword puzzle. She smiled when she looked up and found him staring at her with a lopsided grin.

"Puzzles are kind of my thing."

Baleigh laughed, grabbed the napkin from her lap, and tossed it in the trash.

"I'm ready if you are," she said.

"I am." He got up, put on his jacket which had been on the back of the chair, and reached for the puzzle. She grabbed her coat, put her card key and her phone in her purse, and preceded him out the door.

Chapter 7

Sam cursed as he pulled onto a tree-lined street and into a driveway next to a craftsman-style home.

"Is something wrong?" Baleigh asked.

"No. Everything's fine. Just unexpected company."

"Are you sure? I can catch an Uber back to the hotel if hanging out today is going to be an inconvenience."

"Yes, I'm sure." He unlocked the doors, got out, and walked around to her side, and opened her door just as she was about to do the same. As they walked towards the front door of the house, she heard footsteps on the pavement. He looked over and saw a woman walking toward them. Sam opened the door and motioned for Baleigh to go in. He told her to take off her coat and have a seat and he'd be right there.

The woman was outside the screen door, apparently about to come in. Sam jerked the door closed and asked her what she wanted.

"Well, Sam, that's a nice way to greet company. Aren't you going to invite me in?"

"No. What do you want?"

"Who's your friend?" Sam just looked at her and said nothing.

She huffed. "I have to go out of town tomorrow, and I need you to keep an eye on your son."

"And you couldn't tell me this over the phone?"

"I was in the neighborhood and thought I'd stop by. It's not a problem, is it?"

"No. I'll pick him up in the morning."

"My flight is at 10 a.m. I need you to be there early so I can get to the airport on time."

"Tell him I'll be there at eight." With that, he stepped back and closed the door in her face, and walked over to take a seat next to Baleigh.

"Sorry. I should probably explain what that was about all about."

"You don't have to."

"Yeah, I do. I don't want you to misunderstand what you just saw. Millie is my son's mother. We dated a long time ago. We were together for two years, and she wanted to get married. I loved her, but not enough to marry her, so I broke it off. The breakup *did not* go well. Three years ago, she contacted me out of the blue and asked me to meet her for coffee saying she had something important to talk to me about. I couldn't imagine what that might have been, but I agreed. When I arrived, she introduced me to her husband. She was very emotional; so much so, that her husband took over the conversation.

"After Millie and I had broken up, she found out she was pregnant. She was still angry about the breakup and decided not to tell me about it. The only reason any of that changed was because Jesse was sick," he told her. "He had been diagnosed with leukemia and was in desperate need of a bone marrow transplant. Knowing she and her husband Mark were both incompatible matches, she contacted me, and of course, I was willing. I agreed to get tested, but only after meeting my son. Mark quickly agreed before she could say anything, being he'd always been against Jesse's birth being kept from me.

"The next day, I went to the hospital. Mark met me there and took me to get the cheek swab for the test, then he took me to Jesse's room. He told me he and Millie had visited him after they'd left the coffee shop and told him about me. Jesse knew Mark wasn't his biological father, but he hadn't known that I was alive, or that I didn't know about him. Jesse was very angry with his mother, which is why she wasn't there. Mark made the introductions and left the two of us to talk. He'd cautioned me beforehand about Jesse's appearance, saying it might be a bit of a shock. I thought it was because he'd been sick, but that wasn't the case. Yes, he was sick, but looking at him was like looking in a mirror and seeing myself at his age. I couldn't believe it.

"I ended up being a match, and Jesse got the bone marrow transplant he needed. Thankfully, he went into remission. With Mark's help, I've been able to develop a good relationship with him. He's a good kid, and despite what a bitch Millie can be, she's a good mother. She and Mark have done a great job raising him."

"Wow. Thanks for clearing that up, Sam. Otherwise, I would have thought you were a total asshole. It's good that your son is well, and you've been able to get to know him." During his explanation, Baleigh had been wondering if she should cut her losses and leave.

"That's nice of you to say, but as you found out yesterday, I am not a complete ass, but I have my moments," he said and gave her that cute lopsided grin.

"So, do we need to reschedule?"

"Only if you want to. If you don't mind him coming along tomorrow, I'd like to stick with our original plans."

"Okay." She smiled. "But you should probably shower and change." He laughed and got up to do just that.

Chapter 8

Despite what happened earlier at his house, the day ended up being a lot of fun. They went to the botanical gardens where the trees were showcasing their fall colors, and an art gallery that belonged to a friend of his. Sam had taken his camera along and had taken several pictures of the garden and Baleigh (unbeknownst to her), as well as some promo shots for his friend's gallery. They went back to his house to drop off his camera with the intention of going to dinner. They saw a nearby street blocked off for what looked like a block party and decided to check it out.

It *was* a block party, and after deciding to stay, they had a really good time. They sampled food from various vendors, drank, and danced most of the night away. They'd run into his friend Nick, whom Baleigh remembered from the diner the previous day, and his wife, Eden. Both she and Nick were the same height, and at first glance, seemed to be opposites. His looks were more of a bodybuilder or athlete, and hers were of a librarian. However, the two seemed to be perfectly paired, as they had the same sense of humor, finished each other's sentences, and were genuinely friendly. Sam endured some good-natured ribbing from Nick about being out with Baleigh after initially not wanting to do so. They'd taken pictures with his phone, and Sam couldn't remember when he'd had such an enjoyable evening. His life pretty much existed of work and spending time with his son when he was in town. He found he missed getting out and spending time with friends. He truly had closed himself off after his last breakup. If he was feeling this way now, then maybe it was time for him to work on moving on.

Baleigh thought the block party was a great ending to a fun day. She enjoyed her time at the gardens, the gallery, and with Nick and Eden. They were a sweet couple. Eden teased Sam about being without his camera. Nick joked that Sam's camera would be jealous of being replaced by a woman. As they walked back to Sam's house later that evening, he asked Baleigh if she wanted to stay the night or if would she prefer to go back to her hotel. She opted for the latter since he had to pick his son up in the morning.

"Would you care for some company?"

"I would." She smiled. "But can we make a quick stop at a store on the way back?"

"Sure. Let's go in so I can grab a few things."

She waited in the living room and checked the messages on her phone while he packed his backpack. There were some missed calls and voicemails from a few friends and family members, and just like it always seemed to happen to every woman who moved on from a relationship after being dumped: a text from her ex, Rod. He had been thinking about her and wanted to see how she was because despite how things went down between them, he didn't want her to hate him. He wanted her to text him back and let him know how she was doing. *Not today, jackass,* she thought as she deleted his text. Hopefully, he would get the hint and leave things as they were. Just to be sure, she decided to block his number to ensure he did just that.

"Ready. Is there a specific store you want to stop at?" Sam asked as he hitched his backpack onto his shoulder.

"No, anything open will do." They ended up at a 24-hour pharmacy not far from her hotel. She told him to wait, and she'd be right out. He'd find out soon enough why she needed to stop. She walked in and headed over to the feminine products aisle and grabbed a bottle of lube. Sex had been great with Sam, but he was big, and she was a little sore. It had been a while since she'd been with anyone, and her body wasn't the same as it was when she was younger. She wanted another night with him, and she was willing to use whatever assistance was needed to make it as pleasant as possible.

When they got back to the hotel, Baleigh took a quick shower while Sam texted his son to remind him what time he'd pick him up in the morning. When Sam was done with his conversation, he smiled as he told her she was welcome to join him in the shower even though she'd just had one. She laughingly declined.

"I'll take a pass, but thanks for the offer." She lay on the bed and turned on the television as she waited for him to finish.

Done with his shower, Sam came out with a towel wrapped around his waist. She knew she was gawking, but somehow, she hadn't really noticed his body until now. He was a very fit man who didn't seem to have an ounce of fat on him anywhere. While he didn't have a six-pack, what he did have was a flat stomach and firmly muscled arms and legs—arms and legs she couldn't wait to get wrapped up in again tonight.

"Miss me?" He smiled.

"Maybe." She smiled as she replied, "It depends. Did you bring me something?"

"Yep," he said as he let the towel drop and placed condoms on the nightstand. He glanced at the bottle of lube with a smirk and a raised brow. "Looks like you brought something, too."

Much later Baleigh got up to go to the bathroom and glanced at the time on her way across the room. It was four o'clock in the morning. They had a little more time to sleep before they needed to get up and pick up Sam's son. She got back in bed, and instead of laying down, she lowered the sheet and blanket that had gathered around his hips. She grabbed a condom from the night table, unwrapped it, and put it in her mouth, then bent and took his cock in her mouth. She sucked the head a few times as she rolled the condom down his shaft, then continued to stroke him simultaneously. His erection was quick to appear. Baleigh caught Sam staring at her with sleepy eyes before she positioned herself above him and slowly lowered herself down onto his cock. Once she'd taken him all in, she reveled in the fullness and began to move. As he watched her, she began to play with her breast. She used her Kegel muscles to squeeze his cock as she pinched her nipples. He pulled her forward and kissed her deeply. Breaking the kiss, he then began to alternate between sucking on her nipples, almost to the point of pain, then gently blowing on them. She arched her back and cried out at the pleasure of it. He then grabbed her hips and lifted her off him. He rolled her onto her stomach and raised her up on her hands and knees. He entered and began to thrust deeply in a slow-fuck rhythm. He smacked her ass a few times, which increased her pleasure. She felt her body begin to tremble as he picked up speed. Gasping for air, Baleigh heard herself calling Sam's name as she came, squeezing his cock so tightly, that he had no choice but to follow, filling the condom with his release. The next sound they both heard was the alarm on his cell phone.

"Go back to sleep. I'll come back and get you," Sam said as he climbed out of bed.

Baleigh was tired and wanted nothing more than to do just that.

"That would be nice," she told him. "Are you sure?"

"Yes. I'll call you when I'm on my way back."

She groggily told him okay and went back to sleep. He gave her a quick kiss before heading to the shower.

Chapter 9

It was 9:15 a.m. Baleigh checked her purse to make sure she had everything she needed. Sam was on his way back to the hotel, and she was going to meet him and his son in the lobby. She got off the elevator and spotted them both immediately and made her way over to them. He and his son both stood up. Wow: he hadn't been lying when he said looking at his son was like looking at a younger version of himself. His son, Jesse, was the spitting image of Sam. He looked to be about sixteen years old. He had the same dark brown hair and hazel eyes and gave her a sweet smile when he was introduced to her. After the introduction, Sam asked if they wanted to have breakfast and discuss where they planned to go for the day.

"Sounds good," she said as she moved alongside them, heading to Sam's car. Jesse got in the back seat as Sam opened the front passenger door for Baleigh. She felt a little awkward about spending the day with Sam and his son, but that didn't seem to be the case with either of them. They seemed to be happy to have her along for the ride.

Over breakfast, Baleigh discovered that like Sam, Jesse also had a love for photography. It was a hobby he engaged in whenever he got the chance. In addition to sharing a very strong resemblance, they seemed to have similar eating tastes. They ordered the same breakfast: bacon, eggs cooked over medium, hash browns cooked extra crispy with onions, and English muffins. She also noticed that Jesse was a bit shy. He contributed to the conversation, but he hadn't quite been able to meet her eyes when he did. And when he did, his face turned a bit red. She thought he was sweet. While they enjoyed their meal, they decided to head to the next town and visit the national park because Sam thought she'd enjoy it.

When they arrived, both Sam and Jesse took out cameras. They chatted between themselves as they went through their bags and grabbed what they needed. Baleigh thought for a father and son who hadn't known each other long, they had a lot in common, and looking alike was just the beginning. They were both left-handed and had the same lop-sided grin. She wondered if they realized how alike they were as she watched the two interact. They were discussing lenses and angles when Sam looked over and saw her watching them. He smiled. She returned his smile and walked over to where they were standing.

He was right. She did enjoy the park. It was beautiful. It was early fall, and the leaves on the trees resembled a kaleidoscope of colors ranging from green to red to gold. As they walked along one of the trails, she felt the moisture in the air and heard the sound of water. As the trail ended, she found herself looking up at a glorious waterfall. She'd seen pictures of waterfalls before, but they didn't compare to being in the presence of one. Listening to the water, the chill of droplets touched her skin, and she felt its power as it fell from the cliffs above and made its way down. She closed her eyes to savor the moment.

Sam and Jesse had been taking pictures of the waterfall when he noticed Baleigh looking up at the falls. Her face held an expression of wonder. He thought that it might have been her first time visiting a waterfall. With closed eyes, she looked as if she were taking it all in, so she could take a piece of her surroundings with her when she left. He quickly raised his camera and took a few pictures of her. He was glad he brought her here. It made him feel good to know that he'd given her a first.

Evening came as they made their way back into the city. Sam dropped Jesse off at his home and told him he'd be back after he took Baleigh to her hotel. Jesse got out of the car, told her it was nice to meet her, and wished her safe travels. The ride back to the hotel was quiet. Sam parked and walked her to her room.

"Thanks for the last few days, Sam. I had a good time with you and Jesse. Maybe I can return the favor if you're ever in my part of the country," she finished nervously. She suddenly began to feel awkward. She knew the time they had together was short, but she didn't want to say goodbye. Somewhere in these three days with Sam, she'd come to like him. A lot. She wanted to know him better. She couldn't quite work up the nerve to ask him to call her, but she did lamely throw out the offer for him to look her up.

"You're welcome," Sam said. "I'm glad you had fun. I did, too." He looked down and then looked back at her. "Thanks for the offer to return the favor, but I don't think I can take you up on it. I had a really great time with you this weekend." He paused, looking at her with a solemn expression. "I haven't done much of that recently, and I don't get away often. I know you were just extending an invitation to visit, but in all honesty, I can't. My son is here, and he's my main priority. The possibility of starting a long-distance anything is not something I'm ready to do." He looked away at the last bit. "I just recently ended a long relationship. I thought I was ready to move on, but I'm not. I'm not ready to go through that again. I'm sorry. And, I feel like a jerk saying this, but I did enjoy my time with you, even though I can't give you anything more than this." He reached for her, intending on hugging her or perhaps a kiss. He didn't know which, he just wanted to touch her, to soften the words he'd just spoken.

Baleigh put her hands up as she stepped away from him. She didn't know what she'd been expecting, but it wasn't this. She wasn't expecting those words or the way they made her feel: hurt and sad. "I guess that's it. Thanks for everything, Sam. I'll go pack my things. While I'm doing that can you show yourself out, please?"

Sam stood there as if he wanted to say something else. She turned away from him. "Have a safe trip back," he said, then walked out and closed the door behind him.

Chapter 10

Five years later

Her best friend, Lisa, was getting married. Lisa, Jay—her fiancé—and Baleigh had met in college. Lisa and Baleigh had a few classes together and lived in the same dorm. Baleigh tutored Jay in calculus, and he'd met Lisa through her. Upon graduation, Lisa and Baleigh remained friends. Jay went back home to attend grad school. Years later, Lisa and Jay ran into each other at a conference. They exchanged numbers, eventually began dating, and later, got engaged. They'd chosen a winter wedding in the town of Fallston, Colorado, which was an hour east of Denver. Lisa had initially planned to have an island destination wedding, but after she and Jay visited Fallston last year, they'd decided to have the wedding there instead. Baleigh was the maid of honor. She'd been looking forward to spending time on a warm, sunny island, not on a Colorado mountaintop in winter. She had to admit though, that after seeing pictures of the place and the chapel where the ceremony would take place, she understood why her friends made the change. It truly was beautiful. The wedding was on Sunday, so she'd flown in on Wednesday to help with any last-minute details. It was to be a small, intimate affair. Besides Baleigh, there was one other bridesmaid. The best man and one groomsman completed the wedding party. Baleigh hadn't met the other members of the party yet. The other bridesmaid was the wife of one of the groomsmen, and she was told both he and the best man had been friends with Jay since childhood.

On the day of Baleigh's flight, Lisa sent her a text to confirm her arrival time. She told Baleigh not to bother taking the shuttle to the inn where everyone was staying. The best man had to drive into Denver that morning and had agreed to stop by the airport and pick her up. "He'll meet you at the baggage claim," the text said. Baleigh was not looking forward to riding in a car with a man she didn't know. Although, after thinking about it, if she were taking a shuttle, she would have been riding with strangers, and even though he was in the wedding party, it still wasn't the same thing.

Sam stood in baggage claim waiting for Lisa, his friend Jay's fiancé, to send the picture and phone number of her friend and maid of honor he was to pick up before he headed back up the mountain to the hotel. He had gone to Denver to pick up a new lens for his camera, additional memory cards, and a light meter for his son, Jesse, who would be serving as the photographer for the nuptials. He hoped her plane was on time. He didn't want to delay his start back to Fallston any more than he had to. It had started to snow on his way in, and it didn't look like it would be stopping anytime soon. His phone pinged, interrupting his thoughts with an incoming text. He took his phone out to view the picture Lisa had sent. There was instant recognition when he looked at the screen. He couldn't believe what he saw. *It couldn't be*, he thought. The bride's best friend and maid of honor was Baleigh Emerson, a woman he'd met five years ago, a woman he'd spent three amazing days with only to walk away from her at the end. She was also the woman he'd been unable to forget. He continued to stare at the picture.

How was this happening? Would she remember him? Considering how they parted, she probably would. He only hoped it didn't bode ill for the days ahead. They were both there to attend the wedding of their best friends. He hoped their shared past wouldn't cause any problems. He wasn't so sure though. As he looked at the picture, he saw her hair was longer, but other than that, she hadn't changed much. She was just as beautiful as she'd been when they first met. He remembered how her body felt lying next to, over, and under his. He also remembered hearing the hurt in her voice when she told him goodbye. *Great. Just great.* Well, there was nothing he could do about this recent turn of events but get through it.

Baleigh grabbed her last bag from the carousel and placed it next to her other one. She raised the handle, attached her backpack, which was doubling as a purse, and laid the garment bag containing her maid of honor dress across the top. She reached into the backpack, grabbed her phone, and took it out of airplane mode with the intent of texting Lisa to let her know she'd arrived. She'd been busy trying to gather her pack and getting her dress from the flight attendant who'd been nice enough to store it for her so it wouldn't get too wrinkled, that she hadn't taken the time to text until now. She saw that there was a text from Lisa, telling her Jay's friend, Sam was going to pick her up and he'd meet her in the baggage claim area. She also added she'd sent Sam her number and a picture, so he'd know what she looked like. Baleigh sent her a "thumbs up" and said she would see her soon. Lisa sent a smile emoji in response. She grabbed her bags and took a seat that was still in the baggage claim area, but far away from the draft of the exit doors to stay warm, and waited for Jay's friend. It had been snowing when she landed and could see it was still coming down. She thought about texting Lisa back to get Jay's friend's number so she could text him and let her know where she was when she saw a pair of brown boots and faded jeans appear in front of her. She looked up and stared into a pair of hazel eyes that she sometimes saw in her dreams. *No*, she thought, *this can't be happening.*

"Hi, Baleigh. It's been a long time," he said, his voice sending a shiver through her.

Yes, it was happening. She was face-to-face with a man she met five years ago. His hair had more silver than when she'd last seen him, but other than that, he looked the same. Except now, he was giving off a serious silver fox vibe. He was the last man she would have expected to see. After the way things ended with them, she'd hoped to never see him again. They'd spent three days together, and during that short time, she somehow managed to find herself falling in love. She hadn't intended to, but nonetheless, it happened. He gave her three of the best days of her life *and* a broken heart. What had she done in her life to deserve having him show up again after all this time? *She didn't know*, she thought as she quickly stood up.

"Ah, um, hi, Sam. It has. What a surprise."

"Yes, it is." He looked at her as if he weren't sure if he were glad to see her. "Here's another surprise. I'm your ride to Fallston."

"My what?" Not sure she heard him right.

"I'm here to pick you up and take you to Fallston. Lisa asked me if I'd pick you up since I'd be in Denver. I told her I would."

"Is everything okay?"

"Yes. She just didn't want you to have to take a shuttle, seeing as I was already in town. There's something else I should probably tell you."

"And what might that be?" She was sure he was going to tell her he was there with his wife and kids.

"I'm the best man."

Baleigh opened her mouth to speak, but no words came out. Not a shout, not a scream; one of which she really wanted to do at the moment. Not a sound.

"That was my response when she sent your picture. Is this all your stuff?"

She nodded.

"Good. We better get going. We've got an hour's ride ahead of us, and with the snow, it might take a little longer." He took the handles of both suitcases, whirled them around, and started towards the door. She grabbed her backpack, picked up her garment bag, and followed him to the parking lot.

After loading her things and exiting the airport parking garage, silence shrouded the inside of the SUV.

"I know this is awkward, but we're going to have to get past this. With everything that's planned, we're going to be spending a lot of time together. This is for Lisa and Jay. We need to decide how we're going to handle it."

"I don't suppose you'd be willing to back out of your duties as best man and go home, would you?" Baleigh asked, looking at Sam with a weak smile.

"Nope. How about you?" He looked over at her and smirked.

"If it wasn't for the fact that Lisa would kill me, I'd give it serious consideration." She looked out of the window at the passing scenery.

"We'll figure it out," Sam said. He turned on the radio, and music from the seventies filled the car as they rode along the interstate as the snow continued to fall.

"So, how've you been?"

"Fine. You?"

"I'm doing pretty good. Staying busy. By the way, my son, Jesse, is here. He's doing the pictures for the wedding."

"I'm sure he'll be surprised to see me, too." She chuckled, remembering his son's shyness.

"So, have you and Lisa been friends long?" Sam asked, changing the subject.

"We met in college. Actually, all three of us met in college. What about you and Jay?"

"Jay, Nick, the other groomsman, and I grew up together."

"What are the odds of us knowing the same people? I never would have imagined in a million years that I would see you again, much less be in the same wedding party with you." They continued to talk, keeping the conversation light. Both were still a bit out of sorts. Neither of them wanted to bring up what happened between them five years ago.

The further they got away from Denver, she noticed the snow seemed to be accumulating faster. Baleigh noticed the highway signs flashing *reduce speed limit* and *caution* reminders. Sam reduced his speed as he carefully maneuvered the SUV along the interstate. He was talking less, concentrating on the road ahead. Baleigh didn't mind, as she was still processing what had happened since she arrived in Colorado. Her phone rang. She looked down and saw that it was Lisa.

"Hey, Lisa!"

"Hey, Bibi!" Jay and Lisa had always called her that. "You and Sam headed back?"

"Yes, but it's slow going. The snow is really coming down, so it's gonna take a little longer than expected to get there."

"You guys be careful. Can't wait to see you, Bibi."

"Me either." They talked for a few more minutes before saying goodbye and ending the call.

Finally leaving the interstate, they connected with the highway that would take them to Fallston. The town was on a mountain near a lake bearing the same name. Sam talked about where they were all staying, describing it as "rustically chic," adding they were Lisa's words, not his. Baleigh laughed because that sounded just like her. After driving another ten miles, they were eventually stopped, and were redirected by the highway patrol. When they got up to the patrolman, he informed them that the road further up the mountain had been closed due to a weather-related accident. What was predicted to be a few inches of snow was turning into an unexpected storm with more snow on the way. They were told to turn around and find lodging in the town they'd just passed, as the road to Denver would probably be just as bad.

Sam looked over at her as he rolled up his window after speaking with the patrolman. He maneuvered the SUV towards the turnaround spot and headed back the way they'd come. "Well, seems like we won't be going to Fallston today. Do you have a signal on your phone?"

Baleigh checked her phone and found she did. "Yes."

"Can you look for hotels in the town of Bennett and see if any of them have any vacancies?"

"Yes, I'll check."

Forty-five minutes later, Baleigh found herself walking into a hotel room with Sam following behind her. Because of the weather, vacant hotel rooms in a small town like Bennett were few and far between, which was how she ended up sharing a room with Sam. Thankfully, the room wasn't too bad. It was clean and relatively modern. There was a restaurant downstairs and a bar next door. *It could be worse*, she thought.

She pulled out her phone and called Lisa.

"Hey, Bibi. Where are you? I thought you would have been here by now." Lisa sounded worried.

"I thought so, too. There was an accident on the highway up to Fallston, and with the weather getting worse, they closed it down, so we had to turn around."

"Thank God you're not on the road then. It's really coming down. Apparently, what was supposed to be a few inches has turned into a storm." Lisa paused. "Where are you?"

"A town called Bennett."

"Were you able to find a place to stay?"

"Yes. Seems like we got here just in time. According to the desk clerk, they anticipate the road being cleared and passable by tomorrow afternoon."

"Well, that's good. Thankfully, the activities don't start until Friday."

"Is there anything you need from here?"

"No. I just need my best sister-friend to get here safe and sound."

"Is everything okay?"

"Yes, it's okay. It's just that Jay's mother and her sister have gotten on my last nerve. They have had something to say about everybody and everything."

"Sounds like she hasn't changed much. I guess it runs in the family, huh?

"Seems like it does."

"Well, this *is* Colorado. Maybe you should infuse some of their food or mix up a special toddy for them. It might mellow them out or better yet, put them to sleep."

"Oh, I hadn't thought of that. Good idea. I may do it if they keep it up." Lisa laughed.

"If you do, don't tell them it was my idea. They haven't seen me since graduation, and that was a long time ago. I don't want to make a bad impression, at least not before the wedding. I'd rather wait until the reception." They both laughed at that.

"Okay, I think we're going to grab some dinner, so I gotta go. I'll give you a call in the morning."

"Alright. You know, I'm glad Sam picked you up instead of you taking the shuttle or getting a car. I'd hate to think of you out there alone on the road somewhere in this weather. Tell him I said hi, and thanks for his help." *If she only knew,* she thought, masking the unease this latest turn of events was causing her.

"I will. Love you."

"Love you, too. Bye." The call ended.

Sam could hear bits and pieces of Baleigh's call as he spoke to his son, Jesse.

"Hey, Papa Sam! Where are you?"

"I'm in Bennett. There was an accident on the pass, and they ended up shutting the highway down."

"Wow. You going back to Denver?"

"No, I'm staying here for the night. The road is expected to open back up tomorrow afternoon," Sam explained. "Is Kacey around?"

"She's downstairs in the lounge area talking with uncle Jay's mom and aunt."

"Can you take the phone to her?"

"If I do, you're gonna owe me. You know Uncle Jay's aunt doesn't like me."

"She likes you."

"No, she doesn't. She told Miss Iris that she thinks the reason you haven't proposed to Miss Kacey is because I moved in with you. I bet she's down there now telling her how to get rid of me and get you to put a ring on it."

"Whatever, Jesse. Just take her the phone." Sam was starting to get irritated with his son.

"Don't say I didn't warn you." Jesse handed the phone to Kacey, Sam's girlfriend.

"Sam? Where are you? You should've been here by now."

"I know, Kace, and I'm sorry about that. There was an accident on the highway, and they closed the road. It's not going to open back up until tomorrow afternoon."

"I had a nice evening planned for us." She sounded annoyed.

"We can just move your plans back to tomorrow."

"Okay." He was sure she was pouting. He heard women's voices in the background as they continued to talk and assumed they were Jay's family.

"Were you able to find a place to stay?" Kacey asked.

"Yes, we were."

"Who's we?" she demanded.

"Baleigh, Lisa's friend, the maid of honor. I picked her up at the airport."

"Was *she* able to find a place as well?"

"Yes, she was." He didn't know why, but for some reason, he didn't want to tell her that they were sharing a room.

"Look, we're about to go grab some dinner. I'll call you back after I eat."

"I'll look forward to it. Talk to you soon. Love you."

"You, too. Bye." Sam ended the call.

Jesse watched Miss Kacey as she spoke on the phone to his father. She didn't look too happy. The other two women in the room had been eavesdropping on the conversation and started to talk amongst themselves. They were probably gossiping or complaining about something. He couldn't for the life of him understand how Uncle Jay's dad put up with his wife. Uncle Jay was pretty cool. He clearly must have gotten it from his father. Miss Kacey ended the call with a huff.

"Something wrong?" Dahlia, Jay's aunt, asked.

"No. At least, I don't think there is."

"What happened?"

"Sam is going to have to stay in Bennett tonight because the highway is closed."

"Well, Kacey honey, that can't be helped. The snow really is coming down. At least he's somewhere safe and out of this weather." Iris, Jay's mom, joined the conversation.

"I know. It's just that he's not alone. He picked up that maid of honor at the airport, and she's with him."

"Baleigh, right?"

"Yes, I think that's her name."

"If I remember correctly, she graduated with Jay and Lisa. She was his tutor. She was kind of quiet and wasn't much to look at. You don't have anything to worry about."

"I guess you're right. I was just looking forward to spending time with him this evening."

"There's always tomorrow night. You'll see him then." Iris smiled.

Jesse went and retrieved his phone from the side table Kacey had set it on after she ended the call. Baleigh. The name reminded him of the woman his father had met some years ago. He'd spent the day with her and his father. He remembered her being nice and smelling good. She was also pretty, and he found himself a little nervous around her. He asked Papa Sam about her a few days later. He told Jesse he'd met her at the diner and spent time with her while she'd been in town for work. He'd even shown her his studio, which Jesse could hardly believe since Papa Sam rarely let anyone in it. He'd asked if he was going to see her again since it was clear that he liked her. Papa Sam told him no; they lived in different cities, and they were both going through transitional phases in their lives.

And perhaps the biggest reason: he wasn't ready. Jesse remembered his eyes looking a little sad when he said the last part. He'd wondered what happened to her. He hoped this Baleigh was as sweet as the other one was. The Good Lord knew his father needed a new woman. But Jesse wasn't going to tell him that. Papa Sam had to come to that conclusion on his own.

Chapter 11

Sam ended his call and asked Baleigh if she was ready to go eat. She said yes, grabbed her purse, and walked out of the door he held open for her. They moved in silence down the hallway to the elevators.

"I guess Lisa was disappointed you're not going to make it this evening."

"She was. I am, too. Mostly because we haven't seen each other in a while. She's disappointed because she has to spend time with Jay's mother and aunt, and I'm not there to act as a buffer." She smiled as she spoke.

"Yeah, his mother and aunt can be something else."

"I haven't met his aunt, but I did meet his mother at our college graduation. She kind of ignored us and kept going on about some girl that Jay used to date."

"Ah, yes. That would be Denise Jackson. We all grew up together. Aunt Iris wanted Denise to be her daughter-in-law. She and Jay dated off and on while they were in college, but eventually called it quits. His mom has been on his case to get married ever since."

"If that's the case, you'd think they'd be happy that he's doing so now." They exited the elevator and turned toward the restaurant's entrance. "Lisa thinks they don't like her. She says they've been complaining about one thing or another since they arrived."

Sam chuckled. "That sounds like them. They've pretty much been like that with every woman Jay has been serious with, except Denise. His mom refers to Denise as 'the one who got away,'" he told her as they sat at their table and reached for the menu.

"Well, I for one am glad they finally got together. I think he was in love with her back in school. I was his tutor, and when he found out I knew Lisa, he insisted I introduce him." Baleigh never took her eyes off her menu as she spoke.

"He told me about that. He said he wanted to ask her out but was too nervous, and because he took so long, he ended up being put in the friend zone. Although from what he said, he didn't seem to mind it much since he spent quite a bit of time hanging out with you two."

"That's true. I'm glad their paths crossed again, and they decided to go for it."

"Me, too. I like Lisa. She's a welcome addition to the family."

The waitress took their orders. She ordered a club with homemade potato chips and water. He ordered a cheeseburger with fries and a Dr. Pepper. When the waitress left to put in their orders, neither of them found a reason to pick up the conversation, so they simply sat in silence. When she returned with their drinks, the quiet continued.

"Dr. Pepper?"

He smiled sheepishly, admitting it was his guilty pleasure.

"It's still awkward, isn't it?" Baleigh asked, having had enough of the quiet.

"Yup. Still awkward."

They struggled to make small talk. The weather was a safe bet, so they talked about it and other light topics such as the upcoming activities leading up to the wedding. Friday was to be a sleigh ride through the local area, and later that evening, the rehearsal dinner. The wedding was Sunday evening. A spa day was planned for late Saturday morning, then they would spend the rest of the time relaxing and getting ready for the wedding.

"How's your food?" Sam inquired.

"It's fine. These house chips are pretty good. How's yours?"

"Pretty good. Still prefer chips?" he asked, eying the chips on her plate.

"I do." She smiled. "Care to try one?" She moved her plate toward the middle of the table so he could take one out of the cone connected to her plate.

"Thanks, I think I will." He ate one, then grabbed a few more.

"Well, since you were nice enough to pick me up from the airport *and* you aren't making me sleep in the car, I guess I can share them with you." She smiled and dumped half of the chips from the cone onto his plate.

"Thanks, I'm glad you decided to share. Otherwise, I *would have* had to make you sleep in the car."

She laughed. "Good to know." From that point on, the conversation flowed a little more easily. Each of them also remembered sharing food in a similar manner five years ago, during their brief time together.

"It's still early. Would you care for a drink? We could go to the bar next door."

"Yes, I think I would. I want to run up to the room before we head over first."

"Why don't you go up while I take care of the check and meet me back in the lobby?"

"Okay." Baleigh left the table and headed straight upstairs. She wanted to check her appearance and take care of any needed touch-ups to the little makeup she had on. The makeup she'd put on earlier in the day was still there. She added a little more powder and lip gloss, put some mints in her purse, and headed back downstairs where she found Sam patiently waiting near the elevator bank.

"Ready to go?"

"Yes."

"No jacket?"

"No. It's right next door, so I think I'll be okay as long as we walk fast."

Not surprisingly, the bar was crowded, but they were able to find a table. Sam asked what she wanted and went to the bar to get their drinks. As she sat there, she thought about all that had transpired since she left home that morning. Never in a million years would she have thought she'd see Sam McKinney again, much less have a meal and a few drinks with him. What had started as a trip to Colorado for a friend's wedding had turned into a trip down memory lane—a trip she didn't want to take, reminding herself that she'd somehow, in the short time they'd spent together, managed to fall in love—hard. She hadn't seen it coming and couldn't do anything about it except nurse her heart after he broke it. As much as she wanted to, she couldn't blame him. He'd just come out of a long-term relationship, and Baleigh was a rebound. Truth be told, she'd felt more alive in that short time with him than she had in a long while. The pain of an unexpected broken heart was better than the lonely emptiness that had been her existence up until they met. It felt good to be wanted, even if it had only been for a short time.

Sam stood at the bar, waiting for their drinks, and thought about the unexpected turn of events that had led to this point. The five years since they'd met had been good to Baleigh. She looked no different from when she appeared in his dreams from time to time. He thought about her often. He still had the business card she'd slipped into his pocket when they first met. He'd kept the pictures he had taken, and the ones Nick had taken with his phone the night they'd gone to the block party. He still remembered the kisses they shared, the feel of her body as he held her, and the sexy moans she made as he thrust into her. He wondered what would have happened if he had decided to pursue something more with her. He stopped that train of thought and reminded himself that the feelings and images he was reliving were memories he needed to let be. He was there for his best friend. He was also there with his girlfriend whom he neglected to tell he was sharing a room with a woman he, if he were truly honest with himself, still had feelings for. They shared a pleasant enough dinner and were about to have drinks. He decided it was too much to ponder right then. Besides, he didn't want any tension to mess things up. He'd just enjoy the evening and deal with any fallout tomorrow when they were up the mountain.

"Here's your wine," Sam said as he placed a glass on the table in front of her. "The bartender said the pinot noir was from the Russian River area in Sonoma County, California. He said if you didn't like it, he had another one he could recommend."

"Thanks. What are you having?"

"Scotch," he said as he raised his glass to take a drink. "How's the wine?"

"It's pretty good."

"So," Sam said as he placed his hands around his glass, "you're the maid of honor."

"And you're the best man."

"I am. This day has been a long time coming, and I'm happy for Jay and Lisa. I remember when he told me about running into her again. I don't think I've ever seen him so excited."

"I can imagine. I'm glad they finally got together."

"I remember Jay being very shy when we first met," she told him, sharing a little of her past with Jay. "He was really sweet though. We became good friends. I call him my brother from another mother."

A waitress came by and asked if they wanted another round. They both said yes and continued to talk.

"How did you and Lisa meet?"

"We met freshman year in college and have been friends ever since. She came from a well-off family and was beautiful and confident. I was a bit of a loner, a late bloomer, and very unsure of myself. Lisa used to drag me to parties and other events around campus, and she basically bullied me into taking a semester abroad in Scotland. I was terrified but ended up having some of the best times of my life." She laughed.

As the night progressed, they talked and ordered a few more drinks. By the time they got ready to leave, Baleigh had a good buzz going, and Sam was feeling mellow. When he opened the door to leave, Baleigh jumped back.

"Ooohhh, it's cold out there, *and* it's still snowing."

"It's not so bad." Sam placed his hand at the small of her back to guide her out.

"I'm surprised it's still coming down. It was supposed to have stopped by now." They quickly walked across to the hotel and up to their room.

"Thanks for a fun evening, Sam."

"You're welcome. And thank you."

"You're welcome as well. I guess I'll get ready for bed. I know you said for me to take the bed and you'd take the couch. Are you sure?"

"Yes, I'm sure. It pulls out into a bed. I'll be okay." Baleigh took her pajamas and toiletry bag out of the suitcase and went into the bathroom. Sam took the cushions off the couch, intending to have the bed ready by the time Baleigh returned but found he couldn't. On closer inspection, he saw the release spring was broken. Not long after his discovery, Baleigh came out wearing a t-shirt and matching shorts. She put her toiletry bag back in her suitcase and sat down cross-legged on the bed. She noticed Sam was still attempting to pull the bed out.

"Having trouble?"

He looked over at her and turned his head back quickly. "Yes; it appears to be stuck." He pushed the partially raised mattress back and put the cushions back in place on the couch. He put the blanket and one of the pillows he'd taken from the bed and placed them on the couch. He went into the bathroom and shut the door behind him.

Baleigh looked at the closed door and then over at the couch. She got up from the bed and walked over to the couch and sat down. It wasn't very comfortable. It was also not very long. There was no way Sam could get a good night's sleep on it. As nice as he'd been to her today, the least she could do was make sure he got a good night's sleep. If she was fully sober, she probably would have thought twice about what she did next. But she wasn't, so she didn't. She grabbed the blanket and pillow and went over to the bed. She put the pillow back in its original place and put the blanket at the foot of the bed. She turned the lights to their lowest setting and climbed into bed.

Sam splashed cold water on his face and looked at his reflection as he dried his face with a towel. It was going to be a long night. After seeing her in those shorts, he was sure he wasn't going to be able to sleep. He could still remember what her body looked and felt like underneath him. Yup. It was going to be a long night. He finished up in the bathroom and walked out. The scene that greeted him was a softly lit room. Baleigh, who was snuggled under the covers, looked up at him.

"I can't, in good conscience, let you sleep on that couch. It's hard, and it's too short for you. If you're okay with it, we can both sleep here." She patted the bed. "I promise not to bite. Unless you want me to." She giggled.

It was then that he noticed she was probably a little more buzzed than he'd originally thought. He would almost certainly regret this in the morning, but he decided that the regret would be easier to deal with than a long, sleepless night on a broken couch. He pulled off his shoes, socks, jeans, and sweater, and kept on his t-shirt and boxer briefs. He placed them on the chair beside the bed and climbed in. Baleigh reached over and turned out the light.

"Good night, Sam," she said sleepily.

"Good night."

Sometime during the night, Baleigh ended up laying on her side and being spooned by Sam. Legs entangled, her back was pressed against his chest and one of his arms was wrapped around her midsection. She briefly woke up and went back to sleep. She thought she was in a dream. She woke a few hours later to a hand on her breast squeezing her nipples as it glided down her body. She felt warm breath on the back of her neck as the hand reached between her thighs, and she gasped as she felt the fingers touch her slit. Warmth flooded her pussy, and she felt herself become wet with anticipation. The fingers continued to rub and tease her pearl, and she moaned softly and began moving her body in response. Her leg was lifted, and she became fully awake as she felt the tip of Sam's cock press into her core. As he pushed his way in, her breath caught. She knew she should have stopped him as soon as she realized what was happening, but she couldn't. She didn't want to. She wanted this time with him even though, like last time, she knew it wouldn't last.

Sam was having the most amazing dream. He was making love to Baleigh again. It was as if the five years since they'd last seen each other had evaporated. Her body was as soft and responsive as he remembered it. It was when she moaned as he entered her, that he realized it wasn't a dream, and he really was making love to her. It felt incredible to be inside her again. She was so warm and tight. She fit him like a glove. *Sweet fuck, it felt good.* He should have stopped when he had the chance, but that chance had passed, and he knew he hadn't wanted to.

After they both climaxed and their bodies separated, Baleigh got up and went to the bathroom. When she returned, she came and stood next to the bed and looked at him. He looked back at her and lifted the cover. She got back into the bed, and he pulled her close. He kissed her on her temple and told her to go to sleep.

Morning eventually arrived. Sam looked out the window of the hotel room and saw the snow continued to fall. It was supposed to have stopped during the night, but clearly, that wasn't the case. He checked the weather app on his phone and found that the snowstorm had turned into a blizzard. He was pretty sure they wouldn't be going to Fallston today. Baleigh was still sleeping. He figured it was a combination of the alcohol she'd had the evening before and the intimacy they'd shared earlier. He pulled on his jeans and sweater and headed down to the lobby. He extended their stay for an additional day and went to pick up a few items from the hotel shop.

His phone rang as he exited the hotel shop. He looked and saw it was Jay.

"What's up, man?"

"Not much. Just checking on you. The weather took a turn for the worse, and Lisa was worried about Bibi."

"Bibi?"

"Baleigh. You guys doing okay?"

"We're fine. She was asleep when I left the room."

"Wait. Did you just say she was asleep when you left the room?"

"Yes. We had very limited options for places to stay. This was the only vacancy we could find, and they only had one room available."

Jay laughed.

"What's so funny?"

"You and Bibi sharing a hotel room in the middle of a blizzard. Does Kacey know?"

"No, she doesn't. And I wasn't planning on telling her either. I could do without the drama."

Jay laughed again. "Man, you *live* for the drama. Wait until I tell Nick."

"Try not to tell him in front of Kacey, please. You know they can't stand each other."

"That's true. But anyway, I don't think you're going to be able to head up today. From what we saw on the weather channel, the earliest you'll probably get here will be tomorrow morning. Are you good until then?"

"Yeah. I was able to reserve the room for another night and pick up some stuff from the hotel shop. How are things there?"

"Everything seems to be going pretty well. Kacey has been keeping company with Mom and Aunt Dahlia. Lisa has been threatening to order cannabis-infused food for them, and Jesse has been hanging out with some of the locals and taking some amazing pictures."

"You would think after all this time, your mom would have gotten to know and love Lisa like the rest of us."

"One would certainly think that, but no, my mother and aunt are not wired that way. Thankfully, Lisa loves me despite my mother and her evil twin." They both had a good laugh about that. "Look, Sam, take care of Bibi and yourself. I'll update everyone that you'll be here on Friday morning. And don't worry, your secret is safe with me."

"Bastard."

"Hey, I'm just looking out for you, my brother." Jay snickered. "See you soon."

"Yeah, see you soon." Sam ended the call and headed back to the room.

Baleigh was just getting up as Sam walked in. Belatedly, she remembered she was naked and quickly pulled the covers up around her.

"Where are you coming from?" She couldn't quite look him in the eye as she spoke.

"I went to reserve the room for another night and to the hotel shop. The weather is expected to get worse today before it clears up later this evening."

"Worse?"

"From a snowstorm to a blizzard. I just got off the phone with Jay. He's going to let Lisa know."

"Oh, okay. I guess I'll call her a little later."

Sam walked over to the bed and sat down on the side. "Do you want to talk about it?"

"Talk about what?" She still couldn't look him in the eye.

"Talk about what happened."

"Uh, no?"

"No?" He chuckled.

"Yes. No, I don't want to talk about it." She looked down.

Sam reached over, touched her cheek, and slowly lifted her head to face him. "Baleigh, I'm not going to apologize for last night. It shouldn't have happened, but I'm not sorry it did."

She shook her head. "You're right. It shouldn't have happened. You have a girlfriend, and Lisa told me she's here with you."

"I know. It's just that things haven't been good between us for a while and seeing you after all these years and spending this time with you, although it's been short, made me think about some things."

"Well, I don't want to be one of the things you think about."

"You should. Because right now, I'm thinking about the time we spent together five years ago. And, I'm thinking about yesterday, last night, and how good it felt to have you in my arms." He moved his hand from her cheek to the back of her neck. He drew her towards him, leaning forward, and pressed his lips against hers. She briefly tried to struggle against him but eventually gave in to his kiss and the feelings it stirred up. He broke away and looked at her before he leaned back in. His hands began to roam over her skin and the parts of her body that were covered by the sheet, smiling as he felt her respond to his touch.

Chapter 12

At the Fallston Inn, Jay, Lisa, their friends, and family members all gathered in the dining room for breakfast. Jay had spoken to Lisa about his conversation with Sam. They both agreed not to mention anything about him sharing a room with Baleigh.

"What's on the agenda today?" Nick asked as he pulled out a chair for his wife.

"Not much. I was going to recommend snowmobiling, but that will have to wait until tomorrow. Lisa is going over some last-minute details with the inn's management. The concierge mentioned they have two theater rooms here as well as a game room and a crafting area. So, if anyone is looking for something to do other than watching the snow fall, there are some options."

"I guess things could be worse," Iris said. "Being stuck on a mountain is better than being stuck somewhere else, I guess." Jay's father agreed and said that he, for one, was going to enjoy the peacefulness and catch up on his reading. Jay gave him a grateful look.

"Jay, if the weather continues like this, how is Sam supposed to get here this afternoon?" Kacey asked.

"He's not. I spoke to him this morning. He's not going to be able to make it until tomorrow morning when the roads open back up."

"We had plans for the evening. Now he's going to miss them again."

"No one was expecting the change in the weather, Kacey."

Kacey huffed. It was clear to all she wanted to say more but chose to keep whatever it was to herself and simply sat back and drank her coffee.

Finally, alone, Jay and Nick sat out on the enclosed back deck and talked. "Jay, your mom and her evil twin are something else. Eden said she overheard them giving Kacey tips on how to get Sam to propose."

"I see they're still getting in folks' business."

"Seems that way."

"I don't think they're going to be successful. I get the feeling that no matter what Kacey does, she ain't getting the ring."

"Oh really? You know something I don't?"

"As a matter of fact, I do. And you have to promise not to say anything."

"About what?"

"You know how Sam and Bibi are stuck in Bennett, right?"

"Yeah. No. Wait a minute. Who is Bibi? The maid of honor?"

"Yes. Not only are they stuck in Bennett, but they're also sharing a hotel room. It seems they got one of the few rooms left in the area." Both Nick and Jay laughed.

"Please tell me he told Kacey."

"He didn't. And something tells me that this is not going to end well."

"No, I don't think it will. But I bet Sam is enjoying his time away from her. Jesse said he didn't sound too broken up about not being able to get here last night."

"And he didn't sound too upset this morning when I talked to him either."

Chapter 13

Sam and Baleigh were sitting in the hotel restaurant ordering lunch. Both had worked up quite an appetite. They'd spent the morning in bed together, and now she was experiencing the best kind of ache—one she didn't mind in the least. She chose to ignore the fact that Sam had a girlfriend, and they would be heading up to Fallston soon. She just hoped she'd be able to deal with whatever happened once they arrived. She wasn't planning on giving up details of their time together, but somehow, in every scenario, she conjured up in her mind, that secret got out. She shouldn't be surprised. What was done in darkness always seemed to make its way into the light.

After lunch, Sam and Baleigh returned to their room. Sam grabbed his coat and his camera, telling her that he was heading outside to take some pictures. Baleigh had no problem with that. This would give her time to rest her aching body and call Lisa.

"Hey, Lisa," she said once the other end was picked up. "How's everything?"

"It would be better if my maid of honor was here. Honestly, I think I might be developing a case of cabin fever."

"Same here. I was calling to see if there was anything I could do while we wait out the storm."

"No, everything is pretty much covered. Except for one thing."

"Oh? What's that?"

"Why didn't you tell me you were sharing a room with Sam?" Lisa asked accusingly.

"How did you know?"

"Never mind how I know. But Jay told me. The question is, why didn't you tell me?"

"I don't know. Things were kind of crazy yesterday, and well, I just didn't. But I do have something to tell you now though. You have to promise not to ask any questions until I'm done. And you have to promise not to judge me."

"Okay to both. But let me go back to my room so we can have some privacy. I'll call you right back."

A few minutes later, Baleigh's phone rang. After checking the caller ID to make sure it was Lisa, she answered.

"You slept with Sam, didn't you?!" Lisa asked.

"What?"

"You heard me."

"Yes, I heard you, but it's not what you think."

"I bet it's exactly what I think," she responded, laughing. "Handsome man, dinner, drinks, and a snowstorm. Hell, I don't see how you could *not* have slept with him."

"I told you it's not what you think. Are you going to listen or what?"

"Yeah, yeah. Start talking."

"You remember five years ago when I told you about the time I spent in the city when one of my work trips got extended?"

"Vaguely. Why?"

"Remember I told you about the guy I met at the diner who showed me around and then we kinda hooked up?"

"Kinda?"

"Okay, we did. We had a fling. *Anyway*, we didn't keep in touch, and I never saw him again…until he picked me up at the airport yesterday." Silence rang on the other end, then Lisa shouted.

"No! No way! Are you telling me the guy you had a fling with five years ago is Sam McKinney?!"

"Yes."

"What are the chances of that happening? Are you okay? As I recall, you were into him and a little sad about not being able to see him again."

"That's true. He said he was shocked when you texted him the picture. He had no idea it would be me."

"Wow. It is funny though. For as long as Jay and I have been dating, the two of you haven't run into each other until now."

"I know, right?"

"Are you okay?"

"I'm fine. Does anyone else other than you and Jay know about us sharing a room?"

"No, he told me, and we decided to keep it between us. How has, uh, the reunion been?"

"It was awkward at first, but it's been okay."

"Okay *good,* or okay *bad*?"

"Umm, good?"

"You slept with him more than once, didn't you?!"

"I did," she said slowly. "Do you hate me?"

"No. You're my bestie, and I could never hate you. But this is a surprise. And *totally* out of character for you."

"I know. I also know I've put you in a bad spot, seeing as his girlfriend and son are there."

"Let me let you in on a little secret. I love Jesse, but I can't stand Kacey. The only reason we tolerate each other is because the men in our lives are best friends. Plus, she's been keeping close with Jay's mom and aunt, so that's another reason I don't like her. Don't worry. I won't tell a soul."

"Thanks, Lisa. I appreciate that."

"How's Sam?"

"He seems good. He's out taking pictures right now. He did tell me that things hadn't been too good with him and his girlfriend lately, and he'd been thinking about ending it. I told him if he did, he couldn't do it until after the wedding, since the reason we're in this situation is because of you and Jay's special day," Baleigh finished with a laugh.

"Thanks for your concern," Lisa replied sarcastically. "I do have another question though. How was it? Was it like you remembered?"

Baleigh smiled. If they were Facetiming, Lisa would see the dreamy expression on her face. "That's two questions. Very nice and better." She giggled when she said the latter.

"Although the circumstances are crazy, I'm glad you finally got some." They both laughed. Baleigh heard a man's voice in the background.

"I'm talking to Bibi, baby. Say hi!"

"Hi, Bibi! Looking forward to seeing you tomorrow."

"Tell Jay I said hi. I'll give you a call before we head out tomorrow. Love you."

"Love you, too. Bye."

Jay walked up behind Lisa, wrapped his arms around her, and nuzzled her neck.

"How's she doing?" he asked, placing a soft kiss below her ear.

"She's good. But I need to tell you something."

"What is it? Is something wrong?"

"No, but we may have some unexpected fireworks this weekend."

"What do you mean?"

"Sam slept with Bibi," Lisa told him, grimacing slightly as she spoke.

"He did what?!" Jay asked, not believing what he'd just heard.

"Before you get upset, it's not what you think."

"What do you mean it's not what I think?! He's my boy, but his girlfriend's here with him. I don't want him messing around with Bibi like that. I mean, I knew they were sharing a room, but I didn't expect that to happen."

"Calm down, baby. I told you it's not what you think. First of all, they know each other. They had a fling five years ago. Did you know that?"

"No, he's never mentioned her."

"Second, it was consensual, and that's all I'm saying. Anything else, he'll have to tell you himself."

"I don't know what to say. This is an unexpected turn of events. I knew he and Kacey weren't getting along all that well and he was thinking about breaking it off with her."

"You never told me that."

"You didn't tell me Sam and Bibi had a fling."

"I just found out."

"So Bibi's okay?"

"She sounds fine."

"Baby, you know this is bound to get out before we leave this mountain. I just hope it happens during the reception when we're all drunk." He turned her around and kissed her.

"Do you think it will be bad?" she asked between kisses.

"I *know* it will. Between my mother, her evil twin, and Kacey the drama queen, there is no doubt it'll be bad. But don't worry. We'll look out for our girl. After all, without her, there would be no *us*." Jay tightened his arms around her. Lisa sighed, kissing him passionately. She really did love this man.

Sam came back into the room and smiled at Baleigh as he made his way over to the couch where she was sitting. "The snow has stopped for a bit. I think it's the calm before the storm. There's an atrium downstairs with an amazing view. Would you like to see it? Afterward, I can show you some of the pictures I took while I was outside."

"Yes, I think I would. Thanks." She got up and went to her suitcase to get a sweater and preceded him out the door.

The atrium was more like a very large den with glass walls that went from floor to ceiling and provided a 360-degree view of the snow-covered mountains that surrounded the town of Bennett.

"You were right. This view is amazing," Baleigh said as she looked around. The scenery looked as if it were straight out of a movie.

"Yes, it is." She turned to Sam and found he was looking at her. They looked at each other for a long moment before he turned and glanced out the window.

"How about something hot to drink?"

"Yeah, sure," she answered, looking anywhere but at Sam. Her face and her body had grown hot from the look they just shared. She watched his back as he walked away. *I'm in trouble,* she thought. Sam returned with two mugs of hot chocolate, one of which had marshmallows floating on top that he handed to Baleigh.

"Here's to new beginnings," he said, tapping his mug against hers. "The hot chocolate is spiked. It was highly recommended by the bartender." He smiled. She returned his smile and took a sip.

Chapter 14

Later that day at the inn, Nick and Jay walked past one of the theater rooms as Jesse was walking out.

"Hey, Jesse, how was the movie?" Nick asked.

"It was okay, I guess. I fell asleep halfway through it."

"Up late last night?" Jay smirked.

"I was, but not for the reason you're thinking. I was going over some last-minute stuff for the wedding. I wanted to make sure I have everything I need. Thanks again, Uncle Jay, for letting me be your photographer."

"You're welcome; however, no thanks needed. I've seen your work."

"Aww, thanks."

"You headed back to your room?"

"No, I was just going to wander around a bit."

Nick patted him on his shoulder. "Why don't you come with us? We were going to grab a drink. Since your dad's not here, you can take his place."

"Okay." Jesse smiled. "Do you think he'll be able to make it up here tomorrow?"

"I think so. Jay spoke to him earlier, and he seemed pretty sure he would."

"I hope he gets here early. Miss Kacey is getting on my nerves. She acts like she's upset that he didn't try to get here earlier even though the roads are closed. Like it's his fault or something."

"You two still don't get along that well, huh?"

"No, not really. And I haven't told Papa Sam. He thinks she will get to know me better since I'm living with him now, and that'll change her mind. I'm pretty sure that's not going to happen."

"Why not?" Jay asked.

"Because I heard her talking to your mom and aunt about it."

"See? I told you, Jay." Nick chuckled. "They're trying to get Sam hitched."

"Oh, God, I hope not," Jesse groaned. "I can't imagine having her as a stepmother."

Jay put his arm around Jesse's shoulder. "Come on, son, let's get that drink. You can use that McKinney charm on the bartender and servers, that should cheer you up." The three laughed as they walked to the lounge.

Two hours and another spiked hot chocolate later, Sam and Baleigh found themselves still in the atrium enjoying a nice afternoon. Sam told her about a recent exhibit he'd had of his work. It was not too long after they met that he decided to switch up from photojournalism. He was especially excited about the recent exhibit because Jesse helped him with it.

"He's excited about doing the photos for the wedding."

"That must make you proud."

"It does. According to his mother, he showed interest early on. She didn't encourage him to explore that interest, for obvious reasons. When he was on break from school, I took him on a couple of assignments with me, and he was hooked."

"Nice. Is he still your mini-me?"

"He still looks a lot like his old man, but he's a few inches taller than me now. Or as he likes to say, "There's nothing small about me"."

"Like father, like son?"

He grinned. "I guess you can say that."

She laughed.

"Looks like the snow has started back up again. How about we grab dinner now and go to the bar later? There's supposed to be music tonight, either a band or a DJ, I can't remember which."

"That sounds like fun."

She looked at Sam for a long moment, trying to decide whether she wanted to say what had been in the back of her mind all day.

"What?" he asked.

"What do you mean?"

"You look like you want to say something."

"I do?"

"Yeah, you do."

"Oh, um, I guess I do."

"Are you going to tell me what it is?"

"Um—ah, it's about you. And me. And what's going to happen when we get to Fallston."

"I don't want you worrying about that. I told you earlier, I'd been considering ending it with Kacey, and I meant that. Do you remember when I told you I wasn't ready to move on?" Baleigh nodded. "It was true. I wasn't. Not long after that, I decided to start dating again. I eventually met Kacey, and well, we seemed to get along okay, so we became exclusive. However, as long as we've been together, I've had no desire to take things to the next level with her. She, however, is more than ready. Seeing you and being with you again brought up a lot of memories. I remember how I wanted to be in a place where I could explore what was between us. Whatever it was, it was totally unexpected. I wanted to, but I just really was not in a good place to act on it. I've thought about you a lot over the years. I even thought about contacting you. Believe it or not, I still have your card. I didn't because I didn't think you'd want to hear from me, after the way things ended." He sighed and ran his fingers through his hair. "Seeing you again made me realize why I haven't been able to go further with Kacey. *She's not you.* I never in a million years thought I'd see you again. If you're willing to give me another chance, I want to take it."

"Wow, I don't know what to say." Baleigh found herself getting emotional. She'd been in love with Sam almost from the moment she met him. To find out that he's had feelings for all along her made her heart beat a little faster. "Are you sure about this? What are you going to tell her? More importantly, when are you going to tell her? We are about to be active participants in the wedding of our best friends. I don't want anything happen to that can ruin it."

Sam looked at her. His gaze was intense and steady. "Let me worry about that. Just say you'll give me a chance. And let's have some fun before we head up the mountain tomorrow."

She took a deep breath, closed her eyes tightly to keep the tears from falling, and said, "Okay. Yes."

Sam leaned forward and gently kissed her on the forehead, then her lips, and rested his forehead against hers. "Thanks, baby." They stayed that way for a while, whispering to each other and just being present in the moment.

Chapter 15

Jay, Nick, and Jesse sat at a table near the fireplace. Jesse was glad he'd decided to join them. He always enjoyed the time he spent with them. They were his father's best friends. They'd grown up together, and he loved hearing the stories they told.

"Alright, fellas, dinner is in about an hour and a half. How about one more drink before we go get ready," Nick said.

"I could go for one more. Jesse, why don't you see if you can get your new friend's attention and have her bring another round?" Jay asked.

"Yeah, Jesse. Why don't you?" Nick teased.

Jesse made eye contact with the waitress he'd been flirting with since he'd arrived at the inn. He did a circular motion around the table to indicate they wanted another round. She smiled at him and nodded.

"I swear, Jesse, you're more like Sam every day. You look and act almost exactly like he did when he was your age." Nick shook his head. "It's crazy."

Jesse smiled. He'd met Papa Sam, his biological father, when he was a teenager. And in the time since, had gotten to know him and grew to love him dearly. It made him feel good to hear his uncles say that about him.

Jay leaned in towards the two men. "I have something to tell you, but I need you to keep it to yourselves. Normally, I wouldn't say anything, but I have a feeling that I'm going to need your help."

"Damn, man, what is it?! Lisa changed her mind? You changed your mind?" Nick asked. Jesse looked concerned. Jay was about to continue when the waitress brought over their drinks. She picked up the empty glasses and placed fresh drinks on the coasters. She put a folded piece of paper next to Jesse's glass. He picked it up and read it. He looked at her, gave a slight nod, and slipped the paper into his pocket. Nick shook his head. "Like father, like son."

"Okay, fellas, I'm gonna need you to focus." He looked at Nick and Jesse. "There may be some trouble this weekend."

"What do you mean trouble? How?"

"Sam is planning on breaking up with Kacey, but I think he's going to wait until after the wedding to do it though."

"Did he tell you he was going to break up with her?"

"No, but I'm pretty sure it's gonna happen. You know how he's been stuck in Bennett because of the weather? And you also know that Bibi is with him?"

"So, why does that mean they're breaking up?"

"He's sharing a hotel room with her. He hasn't told Kacey about the room arrangement. Hell, I only found out this morning when I talked to him."

"What? No! Miss Kacey is *not* going to like that!" With a look of surprise on his face, Jesse shook his head.

"No, she's not," Nick smirked. "You think she's going to make a scene at your wedding?"

"No, I don't. I do think there may be a strong possibility at the reception though. Once the alcohol starts flowing and with the evil twins pushing their agenda, things might come to a head. If they do, that's where I'll need your help. This is my special day with my woman. I don't want anything to ruin it. But if something pops off, I'll need you guys to help reign in the crazy. I'm sure my father will help too, if needed."

"Uncle Jay, I'll help in any way I can. I'll also be sure to capture anything that happens on film." He laughed.

"Not funny, Jesse, but thanks."

"Anything you need, Jay," Nick said.

"Thanks, bruh."

"Sam said they should get here around mid-morning. That means they'll be here in time to go on the sleigh ride and attend the rehearsal dinner. The next day is spa time for the ladies and then the wedding. After that, I'll be on my honeymoon, and it's every man and woman for themselves." They all laughed. He raised his glass with Nick and Jesse did the same.

After dinner and some time spent listening to the band at the bar, Sam held Baleigh's hand as they made their way back to their room. Once inside, he pulled her to him and kissed her. Suddenly, Baleigh pulled away, making Sam frown at the action.

"What's wrong?"

"Since we're leaving tomorrow, I was wondering if we should try to keep things low-key between us until you talk to Kacey."

"Why?"

"I don't know. Maybe you'll change your mind once you get there. I just want to wait until you're sure."

"I am sure. I'm not changing my mind. I want you. You're who I want to be with. If you're having second thoughts, I need you to tell me now."

"No, I'm not having second thoughts." *I am, but I don't want you to know.*

"Good. Because after what I'm about to do to you tonight, there'll be no turning back." The look he gave her as he spoke was hot and filled with promise.

"Okay." She reached up, placed her hands on either side of his face, and initiated the kiss this time.

Chapter 16

"Jay, have you spoken to Sam? I tried to call him last night, and his phone went straight to voicemail," Kacey asked. "I wanted to ask him to pick something up for me before he headed up here."

"Not last night, but he did call this morning. He's on his way and said they should be here between ten and ten-thirty, or there about."

Lisa looked at Kacey "Have you checked the inn shop or the stores in the town square? They may have what you need."

"I'm not sure they do. If they don't, I guess I'll have to do without," Kacey murmured. Lisa shared a look with Jay.

"Oh, I saw a cute little specialty shop in Fallston. I'm sure you'll be able to find what you're looking for," Iris chimed in.

Dahlia agreed with her sister. "Yes, we'll go with you. There are a couple of pieces I saw when we first arrived that I'd like to take a closer look at."

"That would be great, thanks." Kacey smiled.

Jesse looked at the twins and his father's girlfriend. In a low voice, he leaned over to Nick who was sitting next to him. "This isn't going to end well, is it, Uncle Nick?" he asked.

Nick smiled and shook his head. "Not a chance."

With Sam at the wheel, the SUV was a mile or two from Fallston. Both occupants were quiet as they drove along the recently plowed road.

"So, we're almost there."

Sam grabbed Baleigh's hand and kissed the back of it. "Yes, we are. Are you okay?"

"I am."

"Good."

"But I do have one request."

"Yes?"

"Can you wait until after the wedding to speak to Kacey? I don't want anything to ruin Lisa and Jay's day."

"I was thinking the same thing. I'll wait until after the reception."

"Thanks." Baleigh released a breath she hadn't been aware she was holding.

"No need to thank me. Jay is my brother, and I would never do anything to disrupt this day. It's been long in coming, and besides that, none of this is about them." He raised her hand to his lips, placing another kiss there. He gave it a quick squeeze before letting it go as he made the last turn taking them to the entrance of the parking lot of the Fallston Inn. Baleigh heard Sam's words, but she wasn't so sure that things would go as nice and easy as he seemed to think they would.

Chapter 17

Jay and Lisa were returning to their room from an after-breakfast walk when they saw Sam exit the SUV.

"It's about time you got here. I was starting to wonder if you were going to make it." Jay laughed as he gave Sam a handshake and pulled him in for a one-arm hug. Lisa screamed and hugged Baleigh.

"I am so glad you're finally here! I don't know what I would have done if you wouldn't have been able to get here today."

"Y'all can catch up later," Jay said as he moved around Lisa to grab Baleigh and kiss her cheek and engulf her in a bear hug.

"It's so good to see you, sis."

"You, too, Jay."

"Jay," Lisa touched his arm, "can you guys help us unload Bibi's stuff? I'm going with her to check in."

"Sure, babe."

"Thanks."

Lisa gave him a quick peck on the lips, then walked over and linked her arm with Baleigh's. The two walked towards the front entrance of the inn.

"So, girl, are you okay?" Lisa asked as soon as they were out of earshot of the men.

"I'm good."

"I'll say. You've got a glow about you. And I'm pretty sure it's not because of the wedding."

"I do not."

"Yes, you do and I'm pretty sure Sam put it there."

"I can neither confirm nor deny that."

"Whatever, Bibi, your secret is safe with me." Lisa gave her an exaggerated wink, and they both giggled.

"So, is the schedule pretty much the same for today?" Baleigh asked.

"No; it's changed a bit thanks to Jay's mom. The sleigh ride has been cut short by thirty minutes so she, her evil twin, and Kacey, Sam's, uh, you know, can go shopping in Fallston. She has some specialty items she absolutely must pick up. Other than that, the rehearsal and the dinner are at the same time."

"Well then, I guess I better get to my room and get ready for the tour."

"I'll come with you so we can talk a bit in private before we go."

"So, what's up, Sam?" Jay looked directly at him with a questioning gaze.

"Nothing," Sam answered nonchalantly.

"Really? That's how we're going to do this?"

"Do what?"

"Look, we only have a few minutes before we all meet up to go on the sleigh ride. I don't know what you're doing. You're my brother, but I love Bibi, too. She's special to me and Lisa. If you hurt her, you and I are going to have a problem."

"I know you mean well, but this is between me and Baleigh. Just know that hurting her is the last thing I would ever want to do."

"Long as we're clear on this."

"We are. Now quit being nosy and help me get this stuff out of the truck." Sam chuckled as he lifted the rear gate of the SUV and removed Baleigh's bags.

They followed the women to Baleigh's room, deposited the bags, and left. Jay and Sam went back to the SUV and removed the gear Sam had originally gone to Denver to pick up and took it to Sam's room. As soon as the door opened, Kacey jumped into Sam's arms, kissing him soundly on the mouth.

"I'm so glad you're back, Sam."

"Hey, Kace."

"I missed you." She reached up to kiss him again.

Jay noticed Sam held Kacey stiffly. He also saw how quickly he ended the kiss, removed her arms from around his neck, and put distance between the two of them. Kacey didn't seem to notice, which wasn't all that unusual since Sam hadn't ever really been big on PDA. Jay shook his head and texted Nick and Jesse and told them to meet him in the lobby.

"Sam, I know you just got here, but could you come to the lobby with me? I wanted to go over some of the stuff Jesse mentioned for the photo shoots he's planning for today's activities." Sam looked relieved.

"Yeah, sure. Let me grab the light meter and cards he wanted, and I'll be right with you."

"You're leaving? You just got here," Kacey said.

"I'm not leaving. I'm just going to make sure Jesse has everything he needs. I won't be gone long." He looked at Jay who was headed towards the door, grabbed the box, and quickly walked out behind him before Kacey could say anything else.

"Thanks for the save, man," Sam told Jay.

"Your ass is lucky you're my brother, or you'd still be in there trying to figure out how to explain to your *girlfriend* why you don't want to fuck her," Jay smirked.

"Yes, well, I plan on remedying that particular situation after this is all over."

"You're really going to break up with Kacey?"

"Yeah, I am. I never told you this, but I have a history with Baleigh. We met a while back."

"Say what?" Jay looked at him in surprise. He'd already heard this from Lisa, but he wasn't sure he'd hear it from Sam.

"I met her at Nick's diner. She was in town on business, and we spent some time together. Long story short—she wanted to continue seeing me after she left. I wanted to, but if you recall, at that time, I was still dealing with my breakup with Angela. You can only imagine my surprise when Lisa sent me Baleigh's picture." Jay stopped walking just before they entered the lobby.

"Damn, man. That must have been a shock. What are you gonna do now?"

"I'm going to do what I was too chicken shit to do five years ago. I'm going to see where things go with Baleigh. I want this chance with her."

"Alright, Sam. I wish you the best, but remember what I told you." They walked into the lobby and joined Nick and Jesse.

Back in Baleigh's room, the conversation was going in a similar direction.

"All joking aside, Bibi, I really am glad to see you. I was starting to worry that you wouldn't get here in time, and I didn't want to get married without my best sister-friend-play-cousin by my side." Lisa hugged Baleigh.

"I know. I was almost desperate enough to see if there was a snowmobile or maybe a dog sled that could get me here. I was not about to miss your day. And speaking of your day, I have something for you." Baleigh smiled, grabbed one of her suitcases, and placed it on the luggage rack inside the closet. She opened the bag, carefully unwrapping the items. "Here's your something blue." She handed her a light blue silk square with darker blue flowers embroidered around the border. Lisa and Jay's names and the date of their wedding were stitched into one corner in the same blue stitching as the flowers.

"Did you make this?" Lisa asked as she unfolded it.

"I did."

"It's beautiful."

"Aww, thanks. Now here's your something borrowed." It was a jeweled comb. "This was my grandmother's. Since it's shaped like a tiara, I can fit it into your hair with your veil. And last, but not least, here's your favorite perfume."

"I don't know what to say." Lisa reached over to hug Baleigh and started to cry. "Thank you so much. These are amazing."

"No thanks needed, Lisa. No crying either. Jay is going to be mad at me if you show up for the tour with your eyes all puffy and red." Lisa hugged her for a little longer.

Baleigh got up to unpack her bridesmaid dress. She hung up the dress and placed the shoes on the floor in the closet. "I need to get my dress steamed. Can they do it here, or will I need to take it into town?"

"They can do it here. I'm going to drop off my dress before we go on the tour. Why don't you bring yours? That we can drop them off at the same time."

"Sounds like a plan." Baleigh and Lisa continued to talk about what had happened since Lisa arrived as she unpacked other items from her suitcases. Next, she hung a charcoal gray tunic sweater in the closet and grabbed black, faux-leather leggings and tall, black, high-heeled boots, setting them off to the side. This was the outfit she was planning on wearing to the rehearsal and dinner later that evening. She hung the sweater to get the wrinkles out, but given its smooth, clingy fit, she doubted they would show at all.

After Baleigh was finished unpacking, she and Lisa talked about the rehearsal. Lisa and Jay had decided to recite their own vows. They hadn't told Jay's mother, who was sure to not be happy about the change. She wanted the couple to recite the same vows she and his dad had spoken at their wedding. She thought it would add a "sweet touch" to the ceremony. They'd told her they would think about it, but in the end, they decided to go with their own words. Along with everyone else outside of the wedding party, she would find out about the choice of vows during the ceremony. Lisa told her that if she wanted, they could take the items she needed to the suite where they would stay tonight, or she could wait until after the tour. Tomorrow was the wedding, and there was a lot to do before the blessed event took place. They had a spa appointment scheduled in the morning, lunch, then hair and makeup. The ceremony was to start two hours before sunset. Baleigh opted to drop her things off before the tour. Lisa grabbed her dress and accessories. Baleigh had known about the bridal party suite, so she had her bag ready with everything else she'd need. She took her shoes from the closet, picked up her room key off the table, and followed Lisa out the door.

The suite was in a separate building connected to the chapel via a walkway that was enclosed in glass. Once dressed, Lisa would be able to walk over to the chapel without being seen or having to go outdoors. The suite was spacious. It had two bathrooms, two separate bedrooms, and a large, open living area. Lisa had arranged for extra tables to be brought in for the makeup artists and hairstylists. The hairstylists were Lisa's cousin, Jo, and two of the stylists from her salon. "You'll meet Eden, the other bridesmaid, a little later. She brought her things over earlier. There's drinks and snacks in the refrigerator for later, too. Let's drop our dresses off so we can head out."

"Here's the man of the hour," Nick joyfully announced as Sam and Jay walked across the lobby. "Glad you could make it."

"I thought I was supposed to be the man of the hour," Jay said, faking hurt feelings.

"You were until this one did a disappearing act." Nick and Jay both chuckled.

"Got jokes, I see." Sam rolled his eyes.

"Yes, I do." Nick nodded. "You good?"

"I am. I'm better than I've been in a long time."

"Really?" Nick questioned. "Why is that?"

"Do you remember the woman we met at the diner a few years back? You coerced me into taking her to the museum." Sam asked.

Nick looked thoughtful. "I remember, but I don't recall coercing you into anything. What I *do* remember is seeing you with her at that block party the next evening. If anything, I set you up for a good time."

"That may be your version of what happened."

"That *is* my version of what happened."

"Anyway, she's here."

"What do you mean, she's here?"

"She's here. As in, she is Lisa's maid of honor."

"I thought someone named Bibi was the maid of honor."

"Bibi is her nickname. She's Lisa's best friend."

"Are you kidding me?"

"No."

"Nick, you know her, too?" Jay asked.

"Yeah. I met her the same time Sam did. He was going to the museum that day, and I suggested he take her with him."

"This is just getting crazier by the minute."

"Jesse met her, too. I should probably tell him before we go. Where is he?" Sam looked around the lobby.

"He'll be here in a few. He had a *long* night." Nick smirked.

"Like father, like son." Jay snickered.

"Both of you are comedians now, huh?" Sam cut his eyes at both men.

"There he is." Nick nodded towards the lobby entrance where Jesse was walking in with the waitress who had slipped him her number yesterday. Jay and Sam looked in their direction, then all three men looked at each other and started to laugh.

"I guess he really is like his old man." Sam smiled.

Jesse saw his father as he entered the lobby. He smiled at the waitress he'd spent the night with and gave her a wink as she walked towards the employees' area. "Hey, Papa Sam!" he called out as he made his way over, hugging him.

"Hey, son. Just getting in?"

"Yeah, Rachel was just showing me around." His face turned slightly pink as he answered. "When did you get back?"

"About an hour ago."

"Did you bring the meter?"

"Yes, and I also got you some extra cards, too." Sam handed the box to Jesse.

"Great, thanks."

"Do you have everything you need for the shoot today?"

"I think so."

"Good. One more thing," Sam said, changing the subject. "Do you remember Baleigh from five years ago? She hung out with us. You were too scared to talk to her?"

"Yeah, I remember. Why'd you have to bring that up? You know I'm over that. I can handle myself around the ladies now." Jesse nodded his head.

"Keep telling yourself that if it makes you feel good, kid," Nick said.

"I remember how nervous you got when that waitress gave you her phone number yesterday," Jay added.

"*Anyway*, do you remember her?"

"I do. She was nice. She smelled good, too."

"Yes, she did. She still does." Sam grinned.

Confused, Jesse asked, "What do you mean she still does?"

"I mean she's here. She's Lisa's maid of honor."

"Wow! Really?! Wait, so you were stuck in Bennett with her these past few days?"

"Yeah, I was."

"Does she remember me?"

"Does she remember you? Did you not hear what I just said?"

"I heard you. I just wanted to know if she remembered me. I remember her. You think she's into younger men?" Jesse smiled.

"Jesse, are you *serious* right now?" Sam couldn't believe what he was hearing.

Nick and Jay burst out laughing. "This is too funny."

"Shut up, guys."

"Sam, you gotta admit, this shit is hilarious, man," Jay said through his laughter.

"What's so funny?" Jesse looked at all three men.

"I'm pretty sure she's not into younger guys. In fact, I'm *sure* she's into men closer to her age."

"That could change. She's only been around *teenage* Jesse, she's never met Jesse, the *man*." He smirked.

"No, it won't." Nick and Jay continued to laugh. Nick said, "Jesse, what your father is trying to tell you, is that you don't stand a chance with her."

"Why not?"

"Because she and I… um, well…" Sam sputtered. "She's just not. And don't try anything with her." Jay and Nick started laughing again. Sam scowled at them and told Jesse to be on his best behavior with Baleigh when he saw her.

"I will." Jesse frowned.

"Come on. Let's get your gear ready for the tour." Sam and Jesse made a beeline to Jesse's room to grab his equipment. Nick looked at Jay after noting Sam's inability to tell Jesse about him and Baleigh.

"At first, I thought he was hesitant because he hadn't broken things off with Kacey yet. Now, I'm not so sure. He seems nervous. I think he really likes her."

"I think you're right. He certainly didn't seem all that excited to see Kacey when he got here."

Chapter 18

Baleigh returned to her room to get ready for the sleigh ride. It was to be horse-drawn sleighs taking them through and around the town of Fallston and the forest behind the inn. The wedding party would be in one sleigh, and the guests and family members who'd arrived early were to ride in other sleighs. Afterward, they would hang out a bit in town and return to the inn to get ready for the rehearsal. Baleigh was feeling a little anxious about both the tour and the rehearsal. She was looking forward to seeing Sam again even though it had only been a couple of hours. Unfortunately, his girlfriend was there as well. It was going to be uncomfortable seeing the two of them together, and even more so, to be with him in the sleigh and act as if there was nothing between them. The rehearsal would probably be worse, she thought, as they would be near one another as they stood in their places and walked down the aisle together behind Lisa and Jay after they said their vows. It would take almost all she had to keep a poker face throughout all that was happening. She grabbed her coat, her hat, and gloves, and went down to the hotel lobby.

When Baleigh arrived, she saw Lisa standing next to a dark-haired woman who looked familiar.

"Bibi, this is Eden Stack, she's the other bridesmaid. She's married to Nick, Jay's other groomsman," Lisa explained.

Baleigh laughed. "Hi, Eden! I thought you looked familiar. It's nice to see you again."

"Oh, wow, it's nice to see you, too! It's also quite a surprise, I might add."

"Same here."

"You two know each other?" Lisa asked.

"Yes, we met a few years ago. It is a *small* world."

"Ladies," Lisa smiled, "here's a little something to help knock the chill off while we're in the sleigh." She handed both women silver flasks with their initials engraved on them.

"I love it!" Eden said happily.

"Me, too. Thanks!"

"Yeah, thanks."

"Where are Nick and Jay?"

"They're getting blankets and the picnic baskets. Jesse is doing the pictures for the wedding, Bibi. He and Sam are probably going over some last-minute details, I imagine."

Baleigh looked toward the hotel lobby and saw the rest of their party: Jay's parents, his aunt, who was his mom's twin, and a petite dark-haired woman she didn't know. She assumed it was Kacey, Sam's girlfriend. Lisa gave Baleigh an apologetic look as the group approached.

"Mr. and Mrs. Washington, this is Baleigh Emerson. I don't know if you remember her, but she went to State with me and Jay."

"Hi, Baleigh; how are you?" Jay's mother asked politely as she shook Baleigh's hand.

"I'm well, thanks. And you?"

"Fine." His mother replied and moved to the side of the man she remembered as Jay's father.

Jay's father smiled. "I remember you. You were Jay's tutor. He says you're the reason he was able to meet Lisa *and* graduate on time. Thank you for both, by the way. Especially for Lisa. We couldn't ask for a more amazing daughter-in-law. It's nice to see you again."

"It's good to see you again as well, Mr. Washington." Baleigh smiled at Jay's parents. She remembered meeting them at graduation. His father was just as nice then as he was now. His mother had been coldly polite to them when they first met as if she was disappointed that her son was friends with Lisa and Baleigh. Based on his mom's body language, that opinion hadn't changed.

Next, Lisa introduced Dahlia, Jay's aunt, also known as the evil twin. The two women were identical in looks and attitude. She responded to Baleigh in the same manner her sister had. Baleigh had never met the woman and didn't understand her behavior towards her. After Jay's aunt, Lisa introduced Kacey, Sam's girlfriend.

"Hi, Kacey. This is Baleigh, my best friend and maid of honor. Baleigh, this is Kacey." It didn't go unnoticed that Lisa did not mention Kacey's relationship with Sam. Based on the frown she directed at Lisa, Kacey must have noticed the omission as well.

"Hi, Kacey, it's nice to meet you."

"Hi, Baleigh, I'm Sam's *girlfriend*."

"Yes, he mentioned you. It was nice of him to pick me up from the airport."

Kacey looked at Baleigh with narrowed eyes. Baleigh returned her look with a slight smile, which was more than likely not the response she was looking for. Kacey walked away and stood next to Jay's parents.

"Sorry about that," Lisa said out of the side of her mouth.

Eden laughed. "No, you're not."

"She's right. I'm not. Here come the fellas. Looks like things are about to get interesting."

Nick and Jay walked toward them, each with a stack of blankets. Sam and Jesse followed. Sam was carrying a camera bag. Jesse held a camera in his hand and was showing something to Sam.

"Hey babe. Ready?" Jay asked.

"Yes. *Please*, let's get this thing started."

Jay looked over at his parents, his aunt, and Sam's girlfriend, who were standing together near the entrance. He moved his head in their direction. Lisa rolled her eyes.

"Eden, you ready to go dashing through the snow with your man?" Nick asked, planting a kiss on her lips.

"Yeah, baby. Can't wait." Eden giggled.

Jay turned to Nick. "Nick, this is Baleigh."

"Baleigh! It's good to see you again. How've you been?"

Baleigh smiled. "I'm good. It's nice to see you, too." As they spoke, the horse-drawn sleighs pulled up in front of the inn.

"Right on time. Let's put these blankets down and get everyone situated so we can be on our way," Jay said, sounding relieved.

Sam and Jesse were standing a short distance from the sleighs. He smiled at Baleigh, Lisa, and Eden as he approached them. Jesse, who had been talking, looked over, saw Baleigh, and rushed over to her.

"Hi, Miss Baleigh. Do you remember me? Jesse?"

"Hey, Jesse. Of course I do." Baleigh hugged him. "And may I say, you've gotten more handsome since the last time I saw you."

"Thanks, Miss Baleigh." His cheeks took on a pink tinge. "Hey, aunties!" Jesse stepped toward them and kissed both women on the cheek.

Sam looked at Lisa, then Baleigh. "Jesse, do you want to get some candid shots of the bridal party and the guests before we get started?"

"Sure. I'll catch up with you later, Miss Baleigh."

Sam put the camera bag in the first sleigh, and Jesse began taking pictures of everyone as they talked and loaded up the sleighs. He took pictures of the family and the bridal party. After getting the candid shots, the bridal party got in the first sleigh with the driver and their guide. Lisa and Jay were in the first seat, followed by Sam and Baleigh, then Nick and Eden, who were in the last seat. In the second sleigh, Jay's mother and father sat behind the driver and his son, who was the guide. Kacey and Jay's aunt were in the seat behind them. It was clear that Kacey was not happy about Sam riding with Baleigh. Sam, however, seemed unphased as he spread a blanket over Baleigh and himself. Jesse immediately started taking pictures of the two groups as they took off.

They made a brief stop before heading out of town for the driver to pick up thermoses of hot chocolate from a specialty shop, then they were off again to begin their excursion. The scenery was breathtaking. The snow-covered mountains, the trees, and the wide, open skies created a winter wonderland. In front of them, Lisa and Jay sat snuggled close together. Baleigh and Sam sat next to each other covered by a blanket. He held her hand underneath.

The couples talked with the driver, the guide, and each other as they passed through the beautiful surroundings. Jesse snapped multiple pictures of the intended couple and the wedding party. He took quite a few of Papa Sam and Miss Baleigh, too. As he took the photos, he remembered his earlier conversation with his father. He smiled to himself as it dawned on him what his father and uncles had been trying to tell him. Papa Sam was into Miss Baleigh, just like he was on the day she hung out with them five years ago. He looked at his father and realized that he hadn't seen him this relaxed in a while. Miss Baleigh had to be the reason, which meant Miss

Kacey had some bad news coming. He found he wasn't too upset about that.

In the other sleigh, things weren't as jovial. Jacob Sr. spoke mostly with their driver and his son who shared many stories and interesting facts about the area. Kacey, Jay's mother, and Iris, his aunt, pretty much ignored the commentary. The sisters "consoled" Kacey. Specifically for Sam's behavior, telling her his role in the wedding was the only reason he had any contact with Baleigh. It was plain to see that she, Kacey, was much prettier and much more accomplished than Baleigh. "Besides, once you pick up your package from the lingerie specialty shop, there's no way he'll be able to ignore you." They continued talking as they pulled in for lunch at the home of a local chef. This was the halfway point of the tour.

The group was treated to local specialties and delicacies. They were to be there for an hour and a half to two hours. The wedding party was mixed in with the other guests. After some discussion with Sam, Jesse took a few shots of the chef and his staff preparing the meal as well as the dining room, table settings, and decorations. Before they sat down, the chef passed around champagne and toasted the happy couple. Baleigh was seated next to Lisa, who was at the head of the table. Jesse was on her other side. Jay's mother and father were seated next to Jesse. Eden was on the other side of Lisa with Nick next to her. The Chef sat next to Nick, then there was Kacey and Sam, with Jay at the other end. Jesse set up additional cameras on tripods and used remote controls to record the event.

Kacey tried to make the most of her time with Sam by touching him whenever she could. She offered him tastes of food from her fork and tried to engage him in private conversation. Sam obliged her, but he did not seem as enthusiastic about the offerings as Kacey was. At one point, he got up to check the settings on the cameras just to get away from her. He knew it was a bitch move, but given

Kacey's propensity for drama, he figured it was for the best. While he hadn't officially broken things off with Kacey, he didn't feel comfortable interacting affectionately with her in front of Baleigh. What had at first seemed like two short days of waiting and pretense had grown into something he found he didn't want to deal with. And unfortunately for him, time spent away from Baleigh and with the ever-dominating Kacey seemed to drag on.

After lunch, they climbed back in their respective sleighs and continued the second half of the tour. The chef had given each sleigh a thermos filled with hot cider. Sam poured a cup for Baleigh and himself before passing the thermos to Nick. He was about to take a drink when Baleigh stopped him and asked him to hold her cup. She pulled out the flask Lisa had given her earlier, opened it, and poured some of the contents into both of their cups. She winked at him as she recapped the flask and put it back in her pocket. Sam smiled, then handed her the cup, and touched it with his before taking a sip. Jesse smiled too as he captured their actions on film.

Baleigh enjoyed the time she spent with Sam in the sleigh. The warmth of his big body next to hers, the feel of her hand in his, coupled with the slight buzz she had from the spiked cider had her feeling pretty good. While she was happy to be in this present space, she hated that they were unable to be open with their feelings for each other. She hoped Sam kept his promise to her. She wanted a chance with him; however, he'd bruised her heart before, and she didn't have the best track record with relationships. No matter how hard she tried, she couldn't shake that thought from her mind.

The remainder of the tour was just as beautiful as the first half. They did a lot of laughing that was no doubt aided by the contents of the flasks Lisa had given Eden and Baleigh earlier. They pulled into Fallston, and the women disembarked while the men returned to the inn. Jay wanted to meet with their wedding officiant to let him know his and Lisa's choice regarding the wedding vows. He was also responsible for helping Nick and Jay's father plan the rehearsal dinner. Sam and Jesse wanted to get footage of the chapel before and after it was decorated, as well as set up cameras in the dining room to get a few shots of the festivities from the rehearsal dinner.

Chapter 19

After the arrangements were taken care of, the group met up at the bar, taking a table on the outside deck. Jacob Sr., Jay's father, ordered a round of scotch for the table and pulled out a box of cigars he had special ordered for the occasion. Jacob Sr. then raised his glass in a toast and told the story about how he'd met Nick and Sam's father after returning from Vietnam. They became lifelong friends, and eventually, so did their sons, Jay, Nick, and Sam. Although both Sam and Nick's fathers were no longer with them, he missed them dearly and was grateful they lived on in each of their sons—even Jesse, who was the spitting image of both Sam and Sam's late father. He told them he loved each of them as if they were his sons and grandson. He looked forward to Lisa becoming his daughter and was also looking forward to having more grandkids or grand pups to spoil; whatever they chose to bless him with. With Sam's and Nick's children being grown, he needed some new ones to spoil. Jay, Sam, and Nick got a little misty-eyed—Jesse as well. Jay's father ended with advice about the key to a happy marriage being a happy wife, and handed out the cigars. They lit up, smoked, and talked until it was time to get ready for the rehearsal dinner.

Meanwhile, in Fallston, the women walked around the town square and visited some of the shops. Lisa, Eden, Jay's aunt, and

Kacey went into the lingerie shop. Somehow, Baleigh ended up outside the shop with Jay's mother.

"I don't know what it is you think you're doing, but I suggest you stop," she said as she looked at her with a sidelong glance.

"*Excuse me*?" Baleigh turned, giving the older woman her full attention.

"You heard me," Jay's mother sneered at her. "It seems like you're trying to stir up trouble for Kacey and Sam. You need to stop before you get your feelings hurt. They're about to get engaged, and they *don't* need you interfering. That man belongs to someone, and that someone is *not* you. I suggest you stick to your role as the maid of honor and avoid any unnecessary contact with him. I love Sam like my own son, and I won't have you messing up a good thing for him. If I thought Lisa would've listened to me, I would've told her to have Kacey as her maid of honor instead of you. Then we wouldn't be having this conversation. But, for some unknown reason, both she and my son consider you a friend, and we're stuck with you."

Baleigh felt her anger rising "What do you mean stuck with me? I haven't done anything."

"You showed up. That's enough."

"Listen, Mrs. Washington, you don't know me. I suggest you mind your own business. I'm not one to disrespect my elders, but for you, I might make an exception." Jay's mother harrumphed and turned to go into the lingerie shop to join the others.

Lisa and Eden exited the shop with small shopping bags in tow. Baleigh attempted to hide her anger, but Lisa, her bestie of many years, saw right through her attempt at a calm facade.

"What's wrong?"

"Nothing."

"Nothing? You're upset, and I want to know why."

"Look it's nothing. Your future mother-in-law called herself giving me a warning. Sam is like a son to her, and she feels I'm interfering with his and Kacey's relationship. She also told me she didn't understand why you were friends with me and suggested I stay away from Sam. She thinks he's going to propose." Baleigh hated how her voice trembled when she said the last part. She knew in her heart that Sam had not lied to her regarding his intentions, but her heart had been to this rodeo before, and she was having a hard time believing him.

"Aww, sweetie." Lisa put her arm around Baleigh's shoulder. "I'm sorry she said those things to you. If I wasn't sure it would upset Jay, I would suggest we both go beat her ass right now for being messy *and* mean. Eden would help."

"Damn right I would," Eden chimed in.

"Thanks, ladies. I don't know why I let her upset me. She's never liked me. I don't know why I should've expected anything different."

"She doesn't have to like you, but she does need to be civil."

Eden, who had been texting with Nick while she talked with Lisa and Baleigh said, "I agree. And you both need to see this picture Nick just sent me. It's of Jay's dad and the boys. They've each got a drink and a cigar. Jesse, too. They look like they're having a great time."

"Yes, they do. And so will we when we hit the bridal party suite tonight." Lisa gave each woman a pointed look. They continued to chat as they waited for the other three ladies to finish up their shopping. Lisa called the inn and requested the driver pick them up now instead of later as they'd originally scheduled. Without mentioning the reason for the change of plans, they started walking toward the center of town where they met the driver who dropped them off earlier that morning and had him take them back to the inn.

"Hey, baby. Aren't you back a little early?" Jay stood in the doorway of the bathroom with a towel wrapped around the lower part of his body.

"Yes, and it's your mama's fault. Although now that I think about it, this extra time can be used to our advantage." She gave Jay a suggestive gaze.

"Why don't you come over here and tell me a little more about this *extra time*? Afterward, you can tell me about my mama," he said as he walked in her direction and wrapped his arms around her waist, planting kisses over her face and neck as he walked her backward toward the bed.

Baleigh went straight to her room when they returned to the inn. When she entered, she noticed a large bouquet of colorful flowers sitting on one of the tables. She read the card and was pleasantly surprised to see they were from Sam. She took the card and held it to her chest with both hands and closed her eyes. Today hadn't been the easiest day, and tomorrow would probably be worse. Knowing that he was thinking about her made her smile. She could feel her apprehension about him begin to dissipate and her head was starting to agree with her heart. She placed the card on the table next to the flowers, then stripped off her clothes and headed to the bathroom to start getting ready for the rehearsal.

Chapter 20

Sam finished going over some last-minute details with Jesse before heading to his room to get ready for the rehearsal. Kacey jumped up from the bed when he walked in. "Where've you been? I've been waiting for you!"

"I was with Jesse. Aren't you back a little early?"

"Yes. Thanks to Baleigh, we ended up coming back earlier than we planned." Kacey pouted.

"Baleigh? What happened?"

"Jay's mother spoke to her about her behavior, and she got upset and was rude to her. There was no cause for it really since Jay's mother was just trying to help. She told her she was being inappropriate with you. And of course, Lisa sided with Baleigh and cut our trip short."

"What behavior was she talking about? She hasn't been inappropriate. She's been friendly, and she's been fulfilling her responsibility as the maid of honor. The only reason she was near me is because I'm the best man, and Lisa and Jay wanted the bridal party to be together as a group for the photographs. You knew all of this, Kace."

"Yes, I understand about the bridal party, but she seemed to be flirting with you. Jay's mother and aunt both noticed it too. Jay's mother was only looking out for me. Now, let's forget about all of that," she said, dismissing the entire episode with a wave of her hand as though shooing the thoughts away. "Now that you're back…" Kacey walked towards him wearing a pair of red boy shorts and a matching cropped camisole, part of her purchases from this afternoon. She pressed her body against his as she placed her arms around his neck. She reached up and kissed him. She tried to deepen the kiss, but Sam stopped her. He pulled away from her and lowered her arms from around his neck.

"I need to get ready for the rehearsal. Why don't you start getting ready while I'm in the shower?" *Yes*, he thought, *another bitch move on my part*. He was regretting his decision to agree with Baleigh about waiting to end things with Kacey. He decided he was going to make her pay for that. And he was going to enjoy every minute of it. As he entered the shower, Sam smiled at the thoughts of just how he'd go about it.

Later that evening in the Fallston Inn Chapel

Introductions were made throughout the group as friends and family members who had been arriving during the day converged in the small, quaint chapel. Once the decorations were up and the candles were added, it would be beautiful and exude the warm, intimate vibe Lisa was hoping for. The wedding was to be a gathering of their closest friends and family members, and she and Jay wanted to convey that in their ceremony and the reception.

Lisa didn't have an official wedding planner, but her cousin, Jem, who'd volunteered to act as a stand-in, announced to everyone the rehearsal was about to begin. The two of them were close, having grown up together when Lisa moved in with them after the death of her parents. He invited the guests to go to the dining area for cocktails and appetizers and then gave directions to the wedding party. He had Jay and Sam take their places at the altar. Nick, Eden, Baleigh, and Lisa went into the foyer and awaited their cues. Nick would escort Eden, followed by Baleigh. Lisa would be given away by her Uncle John, who was Jem's father. When everyone was in place at the altar, the officiant went over the order of the ceremony, which included "jumping the broom." After Lisa and Jay were pronounced man and wife, Jem would read a short proclamation including a brief history of the jumping the broom tradition. When he was finished, the couple would jump over the broom into the "land of matrimony." Lisa and Jay simulated the jump and walked down the aisle followed by the wedding party. After a short discussion to address any concerns, they joined everyone in the dining hall for dinner and drinks.

Kacey made a beeline for Sam as soon as he entered. She didn't know what was going on with him, but she was not about to let someone she considered a basic bitch like Baleigh take her man. Kacey felt she had put too much time and effort into getting Sam just how she wanted him, and she was not going to let all that work go to waste. Besides, in what world would someone like Baleigh get a man like Sam? Jay's mother and aunt were right. She didn't have anything to worry about. Sam just needed a reminder that he was hers and why he needed to let Baleigh know that as well.

Sam watched as Baleigh stood next to Jem, laughing heartily. He knew Jem was married and gay, but he couldn't help feeling a little jealous of him and his nearness to her. He wanted to be next to her rather than suffering through a conversation with Jay's mother, who seemed hell-bent on explaining to him why he and Kacey were perfect for each other and how she hoped to be attending another wedding soon. The last she said with a knowing glance, first toward him, then Kacey. What he was feeling must have been reflected on his face as Jay's father walked over with two drinks and a concerned look on his face. He handed one of the drinks to Sam before excusing them both.

They walked over to the outside patio. With the heaters strategically placed, the temperature was only slightly colder than in the dining hall.

"You look like you could use that, son."

"Thanks." Sam took a sip of his drink.

"Everything okay?"

"No, it's not. But it will be."

"You sure? You were looking pretty annoyed when you were talking with Iris and Kacey."

"I *was* annoyed," Sam answered, avoiding the older man's eyes.

"Look, Sam, I don't know what's going on with you, but you look like a man with a lot on his mind. If I had to guess, I would say it had to do with Baleigh."

Sam looked at Jay's father. "If you were to guess, you'd be right."

"I hope you know what you're doing."

"I do. And just so you know, I'm not doing anything that'll interfere with Lisa and Jay's day."

"I know you mean well, son, but sometimes, these things take on a life of their own, circumstances be damned."

"I hear you." Sam raised his glass, and Jay's father did the same just as the chime sounded announcing dinner.

There was no seating arrangement for the rehearsal dinner because the couple wanted the meal casual, so guests were encouraged to eat and mingle wherever they wanted. Baleigh sat with Jem, his husband, Rich, and some of their mutual friends. After eating, she walked around and mingled with some of the other guests, some of whom she hadn't seen since college. She did, however, notice before and during dinner, Kacey remained at Sam's side. Kacey shot her dirty looks whenever their paths crossed. Jay's mother and aunt pretty much did the same. Miraculously, Lisa, Jay, or his father seemed to always appear at her side when the two women were near her. If she didn't know any better, she'd swear they were attempting to run interference.

Around nine or so, the dinner wrapped up, and the guests either went to their rooms for the evening or headed into town to sample some of the local nightlife. Jay, Sam, Nick, and some of the men did the latter for a low-key bachelor party. Lisa, Eden, Baleigh, Jem, and Rich went to the bridal suite. They were planning on working on the party favors and getting in a little drinking. Good thing their spa appointments weren't until mid-morning the next day.

Kacey, who had been hinting at an invite to the bridal suite ended up spending time with the twins before she eventually gave up and went back to her room with a bottle of wine to wait for Sam. She was pissed. Once she realized she wasn't going to be invited to hang out with the other women, she asked Sam if she could tag along with him. Nick immediately shut that down, stating it was a bachelor party, and no women were allowed. She never liked him or his wife anyway. She was glad she spent the evening with Jay's mother and aunt. They were the only ones who were sympathetic to her situation.

Chapter 21

Lots of laughter filled the bridal suite as Rich played bartender while they filled gift bags with favors for the wedding guests. Drinks were plentiful, and the conversation flowed easily among the group. Snacks were passed around as Jem mentioned that he heard she and Sam had gotten stranded in town by a snowstorm.

Eden asked, "How did you enjoy spending time with *tall, dark, and brooding*?"

"Yes," Jem said, "do tell."

"There's nothing to tell. We were on our way back from Denver when the snowstorm hit. The roads closed, and we had to get a room." Baleigh thought she told that lie rather convincingly until Lisa snickered and Eden flat out laughed in her face.

Jem looked at her. "I thought I was picking up a vibe between the two of you. Spill it! And it better be juicy."

"I can't. Y'all know I don't kiss and tell."

"I don't know you as well as they do, so I don't know that. Deets please." Eden smiled at her.

"True. Let me just say, it was quite the surprise running into Sam again after all this time."

"You knew him before you got here?" Rich asked as he handed her a plate laden with savory potato puffs filled with meat.

"Yeah, I met him a while back." Baleigh's smile was telling.

"It must have been some meeting." He looked at her with one eyebrow raised.

"It *was*," Eden supplied. "We ran into them not long after they met. They looked like they were having a good time."

"We *did* have a good time," Baleigh added.

"That wasn't all you had now, was it, Bibi?" Lisa sipped her drink as she teased her friend.

"As I said, I'm not one to kiss and tell. But it *has* been nice seeing Sam again."

"Don't think I didn't notice him touching you during the rehearsal. He couldn't keep his eyes *or* his hands to himself. Didn't look like he was trying too hard not to either." Jem laughed.

"I'm thinking Jem is right. I don't think it will be long before he gives Kacey the boot. At least, I hope so. Sam is an intense guy. I don't know the last time I've seen him this "normal" and it must be because of you." Eden accepted a fresh drink from Rich.

"Maybe, but the fact remains, he's still with Kacey," Baleigh reminded them.

"Yes, but for how long? Jay thinks he's going to end it," Lisa said casually.

"Nick does, too," Eden added.

"So, do I." Jem nodded his head in agreement. "After what I saw between the two of you, I'm sure it's just a matter of time."

"We'll see. In the meantime, I'm dealing with Kacey giving me the stink eye, and the evil twins all up on me. And Lisa, don't think I didn't notice you, Jay, and your soon-to-be father-in-law appearing out of nowhere every time they came near me."

"I was just looking out for you, girl. I know you're not one to walk away from a fight. Jay's mom came at you today, and I know it took all you had not to drop her. With alcohol added to the mix during dinner, I didn't want to chance it." Lisa handed Baleigh another drink.

"Baleigh has an edge to her. I never would have guessed... I like that." Eden looked at Baleigh with an appreciative gleam in her eye.

Jem looked at Baleigh, then Lisa. "Lisa, I know you are not talking about Bibi fighting. You either have amnesia, or you finally got a handle on your temper. And I'm sure that *entire* last sentence is a lie."

Lisa and Baleigh laughed. The night went on as they talked, drank, and finished filling gift bags. At around 2 a.m., Jem and Rich left Lisa, Eden, and Baleigh, who were more than slightly drunk and laughing.

Chapter 22

"Jay, it's about time you made an honest woman out of Lisa. If you hadn't popped the question, I was going to introduce her to my cousin, Alex." Nick laughed as he teased his brother.

"Congratulations, brother. I'm happy for you." Jay, Nick, and Sam raised their glasses.

"Lisa is amazing, Jay. I wish you both the best," Sam added.

"Thanks, fellas. I am a blessed man. I sometimes still can't believe she's mine. I've loved her for a long time and never thought I'd have this chance with her. I can hardly wait to make it official, and I'm glad to have the two of you by my side when I do."

"I can't think of any place else I'd rather be."

Nick looked at Sam as he spoke, then at Jay. "You can't think of any place else you'd rather be? Like maybe with a certain maid of honor?"

"Yeah, Sam. What Nick said."

Sam looked at both men and burst out laughing. "Okay, you got me. There is one place I wouldn't mind being right now. But, unfortunately, she's not available."

"What do you mean, not available?"

"She's with both your women, getting ready for tomorrow."

"True. They're probably drunk."

"One way to find out. Let's go pay 'em a visit." Nick placed his glass on the bar and grabbed theirs. "Hey, guys," he spoke to the other friends who'd come out with them, "it's almost closing time, so we're about to head back. Thanks for hanging out and celebrating Jay's last night as a free man." His words were met with laughter.

The shuttle from the inn had been on standby, so they climbed aboard, laughing, and talking the entire way back. Once they arrived, the others said goodnight and went to their rooms. Nick took out his phone to text Eden to meet him in theirs. Jay did the same. Sam asked Jay what the room number was for the bridal suite. Each man walked off to their intended destination. Sam saw Eden and Lisa walking out of the suite as he approached. Both women started laughing when they saw him. At closer inspection, he saw they were both more than a little tipsy.

Eden looked at him. "Well, if it isn't tall, dark, and brooding." Both started to laugh again.

Sam looked at both women, not quite knowing how to respond. "Ladies." He nodded toward them.

"Hey, Sam," Lisa responded, wriggling her fingers at him.

Eden looked like she was trying hard to keep her laughter in. "We'll be right back, so behave yourself."

He knew they wouldn't be back right away. He chuckled, said will do, and walked towards the suite. *He had no intention of behaving himself,* he thought as he knocked on the suite door.

"What are you doing here?" a slightly drunk Baleigh asked when she opened the door and saw him standing there.

"I came to check on you and see how you were doing."

"As you can see, I'm fine. Why are you *really* here?"

"I wanted to see you." Sam walked toward Baleigh, reached forward and wrapped his arms around her. "I really, *really* wanted to see you. I missed you."

"Oh, yeah?"

"Oh, yeah." He kissed her. As Sam began to deepen the kiss, Baleigh pulled away.

"Wait a minute, Sam. We agreed to wait until after the wedding."

Sam rested his forehead against hers. "We did. I just missed you."

Baleigh smiled. "This might be the alcohol talking, but I missed you, too." Sam kissed her again.

"I'd better go." He released her and walked to the door. He turned around and kissed her again. "Good night, baby. I hope you dream about me."

Biting her lip, she looked up at him. "I hope so, too." She leaned in for one more kiss. He met her halfway, then opened the door and walked out.

Sam took out his phone as he walked toward the elevator. There was no way he was going back to his room tonight. If he couldn't be with Baleigh, he needed to find another place to sleep. He texted Jesse to see if he was in his room. Instead of responding to Sam's text, Jesse called.

"Are you okay?!"

"I'm fine. Why?"

"First, it's late. Second, I know you were out drinking with Uncle Jay and Uncle Nick. Do I need to come and get you guys?" Jesse sounded worried.

"No. I'm fine. We're fine. We're back here at the inn. I was going to stop by your room but wanted to check first in case you had company."

"No, no company."

"I'm on my way up." Sam ended the call.

That was odd, Jesse thought. It was late. He wondered what had happened that had Papa Sam coming by his room at this time of night.

"Okay, what's going on?" Jesse asked as he opened the door for his father.

"Nothing. I just needed a place to stay for the night."

"What happened? Miss Kacey kick you out because you had too much to drink?" Jesse snickered.

"No. I haven't been to my room."

"Then what gives?"

Sam sat down on the couch. Jesse opened the mini refrigerator and grabbed two bottles of water. He handed one to Sam and sat down on the other end of the couch. Sam took the bottle and drank deeply. He looked at Jesse.

"I couldn't go back to my room."

"What do you mean you couldn't go back to your room?"

"I couldn't go back. Before coming here to Fallston, I was thinking about ending things with Kacey. I can't see us going any further. We've been together for a few years, but I can honestly say I don't want a future with her, and seeing Baleigh again confirmed that for me. It's been five years since I last saw her. I think I might have even fallen for her a little back then." Sam sat back and raked his fingers through his hair. "I was still recovering from a messy break-up when we met, and I wasn't ready to move on. The thought of starting a new relationship left me feeling guilty, because I was still in love with Angela, or thought I was. I was scared to get back out there."

"And now?" Jesse looked at him.

"Now, all I can think is that I can't wait for this wedding to be over. I'm planning on talking to Kacey afterward. I want to see where things go with Baleigh. I feel like I'm getting another chance with her. I just left her, and leaving her was hard, but we both agreed that we couldn't move forward until I resolved things with Kacey."

"Wow, Papa Sam." Jesse shook his head. "I was not expecting to hear that. I mean, I knew you were into Miss Baleigh, but… wow. Of course, you can stay here."

"Thanks, son." Sam looked relieved.

"But I do have one question." Jesse looked at his father. "What is it about Miss Baleigh that makes her different from Mom and Ms. Kacey? I mean, you spent years with them both, and you knew they weren't the ones. How is it you spend less time with Ms. Baleigh, and you're willing to go further with her than you ever did with them?"

Sam let out a deep breath. "I don't know. There's just something about her. Hell, you must have noticed it, seeing as you were interested in her yourself. She's sweet, funny, a little awkward, and she's beautiful." He chuckled. "There's also a hint of sadness about her. I want to make that sadness go away and see her smile."

Jesse slowly nodded. "Papa Sam, you better get to bed. You've got a big day ahead of you. I can't imagine it'll be easy having to deal with Miss Kacey *and* your best man duties. I'll help you out any way I can."

"Thanks, son. Love you. 'Night."

"Love you, too, goodnight." Jesse watched Sam walk to the other side of the suite. He thought about how his life had changed since he'd met Papa Sam. He'd literally saved his life. He remembered when Mark, his mother's husband, introduced the two of them when he had been in the hospital for treatment of leukemia. Jesse had been angry with his mother for not telling him about his biological father. Mark intervened and helped him patch things up with his mother and build a relationship with Papa Sam. Papa Sam hadn't hesitated to get tested and donate bone marrow once he found out he was a match. Mark was a good man, and so was Papa Sam. Jesse considered himself blessed with two good fathers in his life. His mom had Mark. He was hopeful that whatever it was between Papa Sam and Miss Baleigh would work out. He deserved some happiness, too.

Chapter 23

The women in the bridal suite were still sleeping when the knocking started. Eden, who'd returned from Nick's room a few hours earlier, had been sprawled out on the couch. Lisa and Baleigh were both sleeping in the beds. Neither of the ladies stirred. The knocking continued.

"I know y'all hear me in there! If one of you don't get up and open this door right now, I'm calling security!" Jem's voice could be heard from the other side of the door. *As loud as he is,* Baleigh thought, *the rest of the floor can hear him as well.* "You drunks got till the count of three to open up, or Rich is going down to the front desk. One… Two…"

Eden rose from the couch and went to open the door. "Must you be so loud? That's just rude." She walked back over to the couch and sat down. Baleigh had attempted to get out of bed and promptly rolled onto the floor with a thud. Lisa was sound asleep and snoring.

"Listen, girls! Y'all need to get ya asses up! Your spa session starts in an hour, and you have a wedding this evening. Judging by what I'm seeing here, all three of you will need *every bit of that spa time,"* Jem said loudly as he looked around the suite. Rich stood next to him with a drink carrier and coffee carafe, trying hard not to laugh.

Baleigh got up off the floor, walked over, and grabbed two of the coffee cups from the carrier. She handed one to Eden and sat down next to her.

"What the hell did y'all get into after we left?" Jem asked as he looked at them. Baleigh and Eden shared a look, remained quiet, and drank from their cups. Jem took a cup from the carrier, walked over to where Lisa slept, set the cup on the nightstand, and woke her up. "Girl! You are getting married today! Why are you still in bed and snoring like a lumberjack?! Get up! You need to get moving!" He clapped his hands for emphasis. Lisa, now fully awake, looked like she was about to cuss Jem out six ways to Sunday. He stuck the cup in her face and said, "Save it. I need you to get up so you can get ready for the spa."

As Jem talked to Lisa, Rich sat across from Eden and Baleigh. "You gonna tell us what happened last night?"

"No," Eden said, "Not now, but I will later." She winked at him over the rim of her coffee cup. Baleigh tried to nod her head, but being a little hungover, she decided to cut that movement short.

"Nothing happened, so there's nothing to tell," Baleigh mumbled into her coffee cup.

Eden looked at Rich and mouthed, "I'll tell you later." Rich smiled and gave a slight nod in acknowledgment. A hungover bridal party and the angry girlfriend he saw in the dining hall this morning were sure signs there was bound to be some drama ahead. He figured it would probably start during the reception once the drinks started flowing. He got up and walked over to where Jem stood talking to Lisa.

"Babe, let the girls get ready for their appointments. We need to go make sure the hair and makeup people are on their way."

"Okay. Alright, girls, get it together." He gave a poignant look to each woman as he spoke. "If y'all miss your spa appointments, y'all are gonna be one busted-ass wedding party." Everyone laughed at his last comment. The women thanked them for the wake-up call and the coffee as they walked out the door.

Rich leaned toward Jem as they walked down the hallway. "I'm guessing there's going to be some fireworks this evening."

"I'm guessing you're right," Jem responded. "But what's a wedding without some mess?" They both laughed as they made their way to the lobby.

"Oh, my goodness," Lisa said as she made her way over to sit between Baleigh and Eden. "I had no idea it was this late. I could have sworn I set my alarm before I got in bed."

"I forgot to set mine," Baleigh added, yawning.

"I was relying on you two to wake me," Eden said.

"Well, thank God for Jem. He takes his role as the wedding planner seriously. I tease him about it, but I'm glad he does."

"Yeah, me, too," Eden agreed. "I would hate to be a busted-ass wedding party." Baleigh and Lisa looked at her. "What? You'd hate it, too," she told them, making them all laugh.

The men had scheduled time at the local barber shop. Rick, Jay's barber and also one of the wedding guests, had arranged to use the shop so he and his team could provide shaves and any additional grooming needed. Sam was more than ready to go. He'd been arguing with Kacey for the last hour. She was angry he'd stayed in Jesse's room. She didn't believe him and accused him of being with a woman. After all, he'd been out celebrating with Jay last night. It was a bachelor party, but not in the way she was thinking. Her voice sounded like nails on a chalkboard. He'd had enough.

"Look, Kace, I don't have time for this right now. I need to head out to the barbershop. In case you haven't noticed, the wedding we came here to attend is this evening. We can talk about this later."

"We can talk about this now!"

"No, we can't. I told you I need to leave. We'll talk later." He turned and left.

She could hardly believe he walked out on her. *What is his problem?* Kacey wondered. He and his friends probably got drunk and sampled the local flavor last night. Truth be told, she didn't care too much about him fooling around at the bachelor party. Any random he met here was okay, as long as it wasn't Baleigh. As the maid of honor, she was spending an awful lot of time with Sam since her arrival, but that was coming to an end. She was going to remind her of that fact. Jay's mother and aunt told her she should probably wait until after the wedding to talk to Sam about his behavior, but she was just so angry, she couldn't keep quiet about it. Thankfully, he left their room before she said something that she'd later regret. She couldn't wait for this damn wedding to be over. Other than Jay's mom and aunt, she didn't want to deal with these people anymore. At this point, she was looking forward to getting back home and away from them.

Chapter 24

"Umm, this feels so good. I don't know why I don't do this more often," Baleigh said as she laid back on the reclining chair. She'd just had a massage and facial. Now, she sat there sipping a glass of cucumber-mint water as she got her pedicure.

"Because you're a workaholic, that's why," Lisa, who was sitting between her and Eden, replied.

"I work a lot, but I wouldn't say I'm a workaholic."

"I would."

"Why would you say that?"

"Because it's true. When was the last time you took some time off?"

"I took time off for your wedding."

"Before that. When was the last time you had a vacation or even a weekend getaway?"

"It's been a while, but…"

"But nothing," Eden interrupted. "From what I just heard, you are pretty much a workaholic. And you know what they say: the first step in fixing a problem is admitting that you have one." She laughed. Lisa joined in.

"She's right you know."

Baleigh looked over at both women and rolled her eyes. That made the two women laugh harder.

"I do agree with you though." Eden glanced her way as she picked up her glass from the table. "This feels good. This was a good idea, Lisa."

"It wasn't mine; it was Jem's. You can thank him later."

"After last night, this is the perfect cure," Baleigh said.

Eden and Lisa shared a look.

"Did something happen last night you want to tell us about?" Eden asked.

"No. If I recall, you two were with me last night."

"True but did anything happen after we left? You know, with Sam?" Lisa smirked.

"Yeah, inquiring minds want to know."

"Nothing happened. If you must know, we decided to keep things low-key until after the wedding."

Eden thought for a minute… "Good luck with that. I think you'll be able to hold off during the wedding, but something tells me that the reception will be a different story. You know there is always some type of drama with weddings. For the most part, with this wedding, it's been minimal. I'm hoping for the best, but in case that doesn't happen, I'll be sure to have my phone so I can get it all on video."

"Let's hope for the best then." Baleigh raised her glass. "My best friend/sister is getting married. I want her day to be perfect."

Next to the barbershop was a bistro where Jay, Nick, and Sam were having lunch. They were joined by Rick, Jay's barber, and the two men who'd come with him. "I can't believe this day is finally here." Jay shook his head. "It seems like it's been forever since I first met Lisa until now."

"It may seem like forever, but at least she said yes."

"True."

Rick asked how long he had known Lisa. Nick answered before Jay could. "He met her back in college. He was too scared to ask her out, so he ended up in the friend zone." Nick and Sam laughed.

"Seriously?" Rick asked. "I never would have guessed that. You always had it easy with the ladies."

"Yeah, but something about her was different. She scared me and made me feel good all at the same time. I'd never felt anything like that before. We lost touch after graduation, and when I ran into her again, that same feeling came back."

"The difference this time was that we helped him man up before he got friend-zoned a second time," Nick said.

"Well, whatever the case, she's a sweetheart, and I wish you both nothing but the very best." Rick raised his glass. The others did the same.

Chapter 25

Jem and Rich opened the door of the suite to let room service in. The hair and makeup people had arrived and were getting set up. He called Eden, Baleigh, and Lisa over to eat before they got started.

"I'm not hungry. I'm too nervous to eat," Lisa told Jem.

"Too bad. You need to eat so your blood sugar doesn't drop. If you don't, you're liable to pass out at the altar, and we can't have that." After that warning, they each took a seat and ate what they could. When they were done, Jem had Rich call the front desk to check on the dresses, which had been sent for pressing the previous day. Each lady went to their respective stylist and makeup artist to get started.

Baleigh looked in the mirror at her reflection. Her hair was pulled back in a messy bun. Her makeup was flawless with what the makeup artist called "natural-looking glamour." Eden's hair was in a half-up-do. Her glasses and makeup gave her a sexy librarian vibe. Both Baleigh's and Eden's gowns were bronze-copper colored, off-the-shoulder, fitted silk taffeta. Lisa looked amazing. Choosing to wear the jeweled comb without the veil, her hair was styled in loose curls that hung past her shoulders. Tiny rhinestones were strategically placed throughout to give subtle hints of sparkle. Her gown was white, mermaid style, and strapless with a sweetheart neckline. Jem was standing next to Baleigh as she stared at Lisa.

"Our girl is beautiful," he said, his voice thick with emotion. Baleigh nodded. Lisa's eyes, now glassy, looked their way.

"Don't you guys start. If you do, then I'm going to start crying and ruin my makeup."

Jem clapped his hands. "Well, ladies, it's time for a last toast to Lisa as a single woman." Rich handed the women champagne flutes.

"Lisa, love, you are the best sister, cousin, and friend anyone could hope for. How we ended up with you, we'll never know, but we can't even imagine what our lives would be like without you in them. We can't imagine any place we'd rather be right now than watching you and Jay become man and wife and celebrating the love you two have for one another."

"Ohhh, that was beautiful, Jem. I wouldn't be here if it wasn't for you all. Thank you," Lisa said, opening her arms for a group hug. When they parted, each raised their glass in a toast.

"Okay. Let's go! Grab your shoes, and let's get to the chapel! Your bouquets will be in the room off to the right of the entrance. Rich, go ahead and make sure the door to the chapel is closed so no one will be able to get in until we get there. That way we won't have to worry about anyone trying to get a peek at the bride before the ceremony."

In the groom's room located next to the chapel.

"Nick, where's Sam? He should be here by now." Jay was checking his appearance in the mirror.

"He just texted me and said he's on his way down."

"I wonder what happened. It's not like him to be late."

"Who knows."

Sam walked in. "Hey, Nick. Jay."

"Where've you been, man?" Jay questioned him.

"Sorry. I needed to take care of something that came up." Jay looked at Sam.

"Are you okay?" Nick asked, looking at him closely.

"I'm fine. Let's go get this man married."

Jay patted him on the shoulder. "Now that you're here, this is for you." He handed him a box. Sam opened the box and smiled. It contained a pair of cufflinks engraved with his initials.

"These are nice. Thanks, man."

"No, thank you. And thank you, Nick. You guys have been with me pretty much forever. I love you guys."

"Love you, too." Sam hugged him.

"Same here." Nick hugged Jay also.

There was a knock at the door. Nick went to open it and returned with Jay's father. "Hey, boys! How about one last drink with this one as a single man?" He raised a bottle of Macallan's 25-year-old, single malt Scotch Whisky.

"I'll get the glasses," Sam volunteered, going over to the bar and grabbing them.

"Jay, as I've told you many times before, you were my miracle and the reason I'm here today. If it hadn't been for you, I'm not sure I would have been able to turn my life around and be the father you needed me to be. If it wasn't for your two partners in crime, who are also my sons, I'm pretty sure my hair wouldn't have turned gray or disappeared as fast as it did," he said to the laughter of the three other men. "I'm so happy and proud to be standing with you today as you get ready to marry Lisa. I know she was your first love and that you've loved her for a long time. You did something many of us don't get to do, son. You were able to go back and get your first love." He paused for a minute, his voice thick with emotion. "Now hear me when I say this. I know your mom is a little different, but she's been a good mother to you, and she's stood by me through the good and the dark times. She's a little crazy, but truth be told, the crazy is what I like most about her. And from what I can tell about you and Lisa—like father, like son." He laughed. "I hope your marriage is filled with the best of everything and all those little things that make your love grow stronger. I love you, son." Jacob Sr. raised his glass. With tears in his eyes, Jay put his glass down and hugged his father.

Nick and Sam joined in the hug. When Nick and Sam's fathers had passed on, Jacob Sr. assumed the role of father for each of them. He'd given a similar toast when Nick got married. Each man picked up his glass, raised it, and drank to the end of Jay's bachelorhood and the birth of his new life with Lisa. There was another knock on the door. This time, it was Rich telling them it was time to get started. Sam and Jay walked to the entrance of the chapel to take their places at the front. Nick and Jay's dad walked to the foyer of the church where Jay's dad could escort his mother to her seat, and Nick would later walk with Eden down the aisle once the wedding started.

Chapter 26

"Ladies put your shoes on and grab your bouquets. It's time for Jay to make an honest woman out of Lisa! The sooner we get this done, the sooner we can start the party. After all of this, I am more than ready to get my drink *and* my groove on!" Jem said with a laugh. The hair and makeup artists did final touch-ups and once-overs. Once done, Jem and Rich handed the women their bouquets.

Eden and Baleigh took their places at the entrance to the chapel, where they saw Jesse standing with his camera. Nick smiled at Eden, mouthed "I love you," kissed her hand, and placed it in the crook of his arm as they prepared to walk up the aisle. As they entered, the wedding guests turned to watch them. Next was Baleigh. Before walking in, she reached over to Lisa and gave her a fist bump. The fist bump was a habit they'd started in college whenever either of them was about to do what they deemed epic, and Lisa marrying Jay was as epic as it could get. Jesse was right there to capture it all. He had set up the video equipment during the rehearsal the night before to ensure he didn't miss anything during the ceremony.

Being the maid of honor, Baleigh's walk down the aisle was solo. She quickly glanced at the families and friends in attendance as she passed them. When she looked at the front of the chapel, she saw Jay, who gave her a warm smile, and then her eyes landed on Sam standing between him and Nick. Those were three good-looking men, but Sam in a tux was something she had not been prepared for. *WOW*. He looked amazing. His tux fit him so well, that it had to have been custom-made for him. The silver strands threaded throughout his dark hair added to his appeal. He watched her as she approached her position at the front of the chapel. For a quick second, she saw heat and desire in his eyes, reminding her of the kisses they shared the night before. She could almost feel them. As she took her position and turned to await the entrance of the bride, he caught her eye and winked.

The bridal march started, and Jem and Rich opened the doors at the back of the chapel where Lisa stood waiting with her uncle. The guests rose from their seats, and as Lisa walked down the aisle, they smiled, and some dabbed at their eyes. Jay's smile grew wider as she came forward. He looked as if he may have been about to shed a tear or two himself.

As the chaplain asked the guests to be seated, Lisa's uncle kissed her cheek before moving to take his place in the first pew next to his wife. He then welcomed everyone and began the ceremony. When it came time to recite their vows, a small gasp was heard when the chaplain mentioned that Jay and Lisa would be reciting their own vows. The gasp more than likely came from his mother, as she was insistent that their ceremony be traditional. She'd probably have words to say about it later, but what was done could not be undone, and she'd just have to accept it.

After the vows and the exchange of rings, the chaplain informed Jay it was time to kiss his bride. After sharing their first kiss as husband and wife, Lisa and Jay turned to face their guests and were presented for the first time as Mr. and Mrs. Jacob Washington Jr. Jem stepped up to the microphone that had been placed near the wedding party and recited the history of *jumping the broom*. The tradition went back generations. There was a time when it was the only means to secure a bride, but it morphed into new beginnings and the sweeping away of the past. When he was done, he invited the happy couple to "jump over the broom and into the land of matrimony."

Afterward, as man and wife, they walked down the aisle and into the chapel foyer. Baleigh and Sam were next. They stepped toward the center of the aisle and walked behind the bride and groom, followed by Nick and Eden, who did the same.

The new couple spent time in the receiving line before Jem made the announcement for the guest to head over to the dining hall for appetizers and cocktails while the wedding party took pictures. The wedding party would be taking pictures in the chapel, then they would be taken a short distance away via the inn's sleigh-shuttle for outdoor pictures. Jay's parents and Lisa's aunt and uncle were to be part of the chapel pictures, but the outside pictures would be just the wedding party, Jem and Rich.

Alone, Kacey sat on one of the front chapel pews while the pictures were being taken. It was clear she was unhappy about Sam being with Baleigh. It was also not lost on the entire group that Sam did not seem to be bothered by this, but in fact, seemed relaxed and comfortable. She was also not happy being excluded from going along on the outdoor wedding shoot. She didn't see why she couldn't go, and she thought the excuse Jesse gave her was flimsy at best; *because the sleigh wasn't big enough.* Contrary to what Jesse said, there should have been room for her. Yes, she was most definitely going to talk with Sam. She felt like he was ignoring her. The more she thought about it, the choice became clear. She'd do it when he returned to the dining hall for the reception.

Sam was glad they were pretty much done with the indoor pictures. The wedding had been a little more challenging than he thought it would be. Baleigh had captured his full attention the moment she stepped into the chapel. He could hardly take his eyes off her. The fact that he managed to do so was a pure feat of strength. He couldn't stop himself winking at her as they turned to watch the entrance of the bride. Posing for pictures was yet another feat of strength. As he stood next to her, he'd wanted more than just her hand in the crook of his arm or his hand at the small of her back. With Kacey sitting front row and center, shooting daggers at Baleigh, he managed to restrain himself—barely. Thankfully, they finished in the chapel and got ready to go to the outdoor site. The women grabbed their matching faux fur stoles and walked in the direction of the lobby where the shuttle waited. Sam didn't follow them immediately; he was in the midst of a heated discussion with Kacey.

"We need to talk," she hissed.

"Can it wait until after the reception?"

"I guess it will have to." She huffed and then walked away.

Sam jogged across the lobby to catch up with the rest of the group. Even though it would be for a short time, he looked forward to being with Baleigh, having a drink, and maybe sharing a few laughs as they rode to the photo site. He'd have to remember to commend Jesse for the outdoor shoot suggestion. The surrounding scenery was too beautiful to not include in the wedding pictures.

The wedding party got into the sleigh that would serve as their transportation. Before they pulled away from the inn, Jem draped a white faux stole around Lisa's shoulders. Each member of the wedding party had lap blankets embroidered with the wedding date along with Lisa and Jay's names. Jesse snapped pictures of the party before they headed off a short distance to an area just at the entrance of the surrounding forest where both the trees and the mountains could be seen.

Once they arrived, Jesse took pictures of the bride and groom, and then of the entire wedding party. Some were standard types with smiles, some with crazy poses, and then he had the sleigh driver bring out the champagne he'd stashed and had captured pictures of them all sharing a toast. In between shots, he noticed Papa Sam and Miss Baleigh. He loved seeing his father look so happy. He also noticed he seemed to touch Miss Baleigh every chance he got; surprising since he wasn't given to public shows of affection. She didn't seem to mind though. Jesse was able to get a few shots of them when they thought no one was looking. As he viewed the pictures he'd taken of them, he couldn't help but feel a little bit sorry for Kacey. There was no way Papa Sam was going to propose. But then, he remembered she didn't really care for him. *Oh, well*, he thought. *If Kacey cared about his Papa Sam as she claimed, her relationship with me would be a little better.* He took a few more snapshots and was taking some additional ones of the surrounding area when Sam walked up to him.

"Hey, son. Lisa and Jay want to get a picture with you."

"Okay," he said, handing his camera to his dad and going over to where they were standing. Both Lisa and Jay got on either side of him, and Sam snapped a few pictures.

Eden came over and took the camera from Sam so she could get a picture of him and the men, then called Baleigh over and snapped a picture of her with Sam and Jesse. She gave the camera back to Jesse, gave Sam a look, and said, "You can thank me later," as she winked at him.

The group enjoyed one more glass of champagne before heading back to the inn. During the ride, Sam grabbed Baleigh's hand and kissed it. Baleigh felt a thrill. The touch of his lips seemed to travel up her arm and go directly to her heart. She also felt a twinge of fear and self-doubt. This all seemed to be too good to be true. She was happy, and for the first time in a long time, there was a relationship on the horizon. She wanted to be with Sam, but he still hadn't ended things with Kacey. She wanted to believe him wholeheartedly, but she couldn't commit one hundred percent until he did. Despite Sam seeming committed to giving them a chance, she still had to deal with his angry girlfriend and the evil twins.

She really should have called Sam on his affectionate behavior, but she couldn't even if she'd wanted to. He hadn't officially broken it off with Kacey yet, but Baleigh didn't care. She'd fallen back in love with him. Just like before, she'd fallen quickly, which made her feel nervous and on edge. If he didn't come through on his promise to her, she didn't think she'd recover this time.

Sam was quiet on the way back as he watched different emotions play across Baleigh's face. He doubted she knew how transparent her feelings were and was surprised at himself for even noticing. Since being here and being with Baleigh again, he found himself experiencing feelings he'd long since forgotten, —feelings he hadn't had with Kacey or any other woman in a very long time. This was the first time in his life he'd ever looked forward to ending a relationship. He hated the thought of hurting Kacey, but he couldn't stand the thought of not being with Baleigh. He also couldn't stomach the thought of her with another man. Yeah, he was gone. But he was fine with being gone so long as Baleigh was with him.

Chapter 27

"Attention, please. Ladies and gentlemen, may I present to you, the wedding party," Jem said from the DJ booth.

"Nicholas and Eden Stack." The couple walked in, and when they reached the center of the room, she curtsied, and he bowed and kissed her hand. Both straightened, smiled at the guests, and walked over to the wedding table.

"Samuel McKinney and Baleigh Emerson." Sam placed her hand in the crook of his elbow as they walked to the center of the room. He then spun her around in a circle. Baleigh looked surprised and laughed. Sam smiled and led her by the hand over to the wedding table.

"And now, everyone, it is with great pleasure that I present to you Mr. and Mrs. Jacob Washington, Jr." Everyone clapped and began to tap their spoons against their glass. Jay smiled as he kissed Lisa before heading over to take their place on the dais.

After the blessing of the meal, the waitstaff began to serve the first course. Eden looked over at Baleigh with a teasing gleam in her eye. "I didn't know you were a dancer." She smirked.

Baleigh looked at her, and to her surprise, she giggled, which caused Eden to do the same. "That was a surprise. It was kind of fun though." The server for their table politely interrupted them and asked their wine preference.

After he poured their wine, Eden turned to Baleigh. "Tall, dark, and brooding is full of surprises. I wonder what other tricks he's got hidden up his sleeve. You're a good influence on him."

"I don't know about that. Maybe it's the altitude of this place or the amount of alcohol he's consumed."

"Keep thinking that if it makes you feel better." She raised her wine glass in a silent toast and took a sip.

Maybe I am lying to myself, Baleigh thought. She turned away from Eden and noticed a very angry Kacey staring at her from where she sat with the evil twins. The twins were giving her the stink eye as well. Baleigh raised her wine glass, and the server refilled it.

After the meal was finished, the servers went around the tables with champagne flutes. Jem stood next to the mic stand and called Lisa's uncle John up for remarks, then Jay's father. When Jay's father finished, he called Baleigh.

Baleigh stood and smiled as she went to stand in front of the microphone. She looked over at Lisa and Jay and began to share what was in her heart. "Lisa, when we met at State, your friendship was a blessing to a scared young girl who left home to attend college and find her place in the world. You were then, as you are now, beautiful, confident, and one of the nicest people I'd ever known. Jay, when I got assigned as your peer tutor for calculus, we hit it off instantly. I still remember when you found out that Lisa and I were friends, and you talked me into introducing you to her. I did, but you never worked up the nerve to ask her out. Instead, you became a good friend to us both; so much so, that it was rare not to see the three of us together around campus. We graduated, and time moved on as we each went on to live our lives. Lisa and I remained best friends, but as it sometimes happens in life, we lost contact with Jay. Then one night, three years ago, I got a call from Lisa. She'd run into you at a tradeshow. She was *very* happy to see you, and she went on about how sweet you were. It was also not lost on her that you were a "full-grown, sexy-ass man." Her words, not mine." This was met with laughter. "Turns out that in addition to becoming a successful entrepreneur, you'd also gotten over that case of nerves that prevented you from asking Lisa out when we were in college. Fast forward, and here we are. Lisa and Jay, I am so happy for you. You two are the brother and sister I never had. I love you both and wish you the very best." Baleigh raised her glass to toast the happy couple.

Jem introduced Sam. Sam rose from his seat and watched Baleigh retake hers as he made his way to the microphone. "It has truly been a joy to be present this day and see my brother join with Lisa, the love of his life. I remember when Nick, Jay, and I were home from school on summer break one year, and we were at the lake. We were catching up since we'd all gone in different directions after high school. Jay told us he'd met "the one." We teased him about it, but we were secretly envious, as we hoped to do the same. He told us her name was Lisa, and that she was sweet and beautiful, and she made him nervous. Being the good brothers that we were, we encouraged him to ask her out once school was back in session. Jay never got around to asking Lisa out and found himself frustrated and in the friend zone. A few years ago, he told us he'd run into Lisa at a business conference. This time he decided to man up and shoot his shot." Everyone laughed. "I'm glad you got your act together man. Lisa is a treasure and a welcome addition to the family. I love you both and wish you a lifetime of happiness. Cheers!"

Chapter 28

"Mr. & Mrs. Jacob Washington, Jr." Jem removed the mic from the stand and handed it to Jay.

"We'd like to thank each one of you for sharing our day. We love you and hope that you're enjoying your time here. Without further ado, let's get this party started."

The DJ took over from there. "Attention please," he called out. "It's time for the first dance of the bride and groom." Lisa and Jay took to the dance floor, holding hands. They danced to *Softly Whispering I Love You* by Paul Young. It was the first song they'd danced to when they'd attended a campus party while in college. That song was followed up with a cover version of Stevie Wonder's *As*, by George Michael and Mary J. Blige.

When the first verse ended and the chorus began, the DJ called for the rest of the wedding party to join in. Nick, Eden, Sam, and Baleigh joined Lisa and Jay on the dance floor. The song played on, and the DJ called for the parents to join them. When all the photographs were taken, he opened the floor to everyone else. The song ended, and he began to play the reception music playlist. The wedding party and guests continued to dance. The bride and groom left the floor shortly after and began to make their rounds. Kacey made her way over to where Sam and Baleigh had been dancing. Baleigh had seen her approaching and excused herself. She left the floor and headed to the restroom.

Leaving the restroom, she bumped into Jesse. She was so focused on heading to the bar, she wasn't paying attention.

"Sorry Jesse."

Jesse grabbed her arms to steady her. "No problem." He smiled. "Where's the fire?"

"No fire, just not paying attention. I was heading to the bar."

"Mind if I join you?"

"No, not at all."

"In that case, allow me." Jesse held out his arm and walked with her to the nearest bar. "What are you having?"

"Bourbon. Neat." Jesse raised his eyebrows at that and turned and gave their order to the waiting bartender.

"Bourbon, huh?"

"Yes. I bet you were expecting me to order something cute and sweet, weren't you?"

"I was. Other than my Nana and Aunt Lisa, I don't know of any other women who drink bourbon. You probably smoke cigars, too, don't you?"

Baleigh laughed, nodding. "Yes, I've been known to on occasion."

"You and Aunt Lisa are grown and sexy women. That's what my grandfather says about my Nana. I didn't understand what he was saying when I was younger. I do now, though."

"Aww, Jesse, that's sweet of you to say."

"Here ya go." The bartender placed their drinks on the bar. Jesse handed Baleigh hers after placing a dollar in the tip jar, and then picked up his beer.

"I'm taking a little break. Care to keep me company for a bit? I'll try not to flirt with you or say anything inappropriate, but I'm not making any promises." He smiled, and at that moment, he looked so much like Sam, that Baleigh almost sighed. She caught herself and laughed.

"Okay, but if you get out of hand, I can't be responsible for my actions. I'd hate to have to mess up that pretty face, however, I will fight at a wedding reception—best friend's or not," she told him, sending them both into a fit of laughter. They continued to talk and laugh as they watched the guests on the dance floor. Everyone seemed to be having a good time. Lisa and Jay were radiant with happiness, and Nick and Eden were still on the dance floor. There was no sign of Sam and Kacey. Baleigh pretended not to notice that he was missing. Not long after, Jesse went back to taking pictures, and she danced with Nick and Eden, friends from college, and some of the other guests.

A little later in the evening, the DJ announced that it was time for the bride and groom to cut the cake. Everyone gathered closely around the table to watch. She'd been standing next to Nick and Eden when she felt the warmth of a hand on the small of her back. It was only there briefly, but she didn't have to turn her head to see who touched her. She'd smelled his cologne and felt his presence. She looked to her right and watched as Sam stood beside her. He smiled at her and was about to speak when Jay's aunt Dahlia pushed her way to stand in between them.

"Isn't that a beautiful cake?" She looked at Baleigh as she spoke. "I wonder what flavors they chose for the layers?"

Kacey, who was standing on the other side of Sam, leaned forward and smirked at Baleigh. It had been crystal clear since she'd arrived that the evil twins were Team Kacey, but she was getting tired of their attitudes and death glares. Combined with her fears about her and Sam, her emotions were starting to get the better of her. She'd been enjoying herself, but as the evening wore on, she was starting to fray at the edges a bit. It was hard to watch Sam with Kacey. She trusted him to keep his promise to her, but she couldn't stop thinking about him walking away from her five years ago. She looked over at Lisa and Jay radiating happiness as they fed each other pieces of cake. This evening *really* needed to be over soon.

Lisa walked out to the dance floor with Jem. She held her bouquet, which signaled the part of the wedding reception Baleigh hated most. Jem spoke into the mic.

"Now, will all of the single ladies please gather on the dance floor?"

Baleigh groaned. Eden, who'd been standing next to her, grinned knowingly.

"What's that you say? You've been looking forward to this all evening?"

"No, that's not what I said, and you know it."

"Yeah, I know. I always hated this part, too. You better get on out there before Jem calls you out."

"Knowing him, he definitely will."

Eden grabbed a champagne flute from a passing server and handed it to Baleigh. "Drink up and put on your dragon panties. You got this!" Baleigh, laughing, accepted the glass, giving Eden a look.

"Dragon panties? Is that a thing?"

"I just made it up." She hunched her shoulders. "Dragons are fierce and don't hide from evil twins or bitchy ex-girlfriends. You can thank me later. Cheers!" She winked. Baleigh drank and passed the empty glass back to Eden.

"Thanks for the pep talk." She smoothed her dress, doing a little shimmy, and squared her shoulders before she walked out to join the other women on the floor. She noticed Kacey was there as well, standing in front of the group on the opposite side of her. The woman let her hatred of Baleigh show for a few seconds before she quickly turned away.

"One, two, and three!" Jem shouted joyfully. Baleigh hadn't even made it across the dance floor to where the others had gathered when she heard him. She looked over to where he was standing next to Lisa and saw the bouquet headed toward her. For a split second, she thought about moving away from it, but she quickly nixed that notion and reached out to catch it. As far and as hard as Lisa tossed it, it would have hit her in the face before it fell to the floor. After catching it, she glared at Lisa who was smiling from ear to ear, giving her a slight shrug before walking over to take her seat so Jay could remove her garter. Jem avoided looking at her, but she could hear the laughter in his voice as he invited the unmarried men to come forward. When Baleigh glanced over at Eden, she saw both she and Nick looking back at her laughing. Catching the bouquet had not been on her list of things to do today. She had hoped to have been in the ladies' room or perhaps outside getting some air when the time came for the bouquet toss. Given how things had been going during the last hour or so, she shouldn't have been surprised. This day was taking a turn.

Rich walked over with two glasses. "You should have seen the look on your face when you saw that bouquet coming in your direction. I hope Jesse got a picture."

"Not funny, Rich." Baleigh narrowed her eyes at him.

"It was funny as hell to whoever was watching." He laughed. "Here you go. I figured you might want a drink after almost being taken out by a flying bouquet."

"Alright, it was funny. I was hoping to hide in the back of the group and go unnoticed. Who knew Lisa could toss a bunch of flowers like that? I swear it was about to hit me in the face," she said before laughing herself, taking a sip from the champagne flute Rich had handed her.

They clinked glasses and watched as Jay reached under Lisa's dress to remove the garter from her leg. His hands moved slowly down her leg, and he smiled as he grabbed her shoe to remove it and slide the garter over her foot. "Keep it PG, Jay!" someone jokingly called out. Everyone laughed except the evil twins. Jay's aunt leaned over and said something to his mother. Both women focused on Lisa with matching looks of disgust.

"Okay, fellas!" Jem said. "Your turn." He covered the mic with his hand and leaned over to Jesse who was standing next to him. "You want in on this?"

"I would, but there is no way I'm going to miss getting this," he replied, chuckling. "I wonder who's going to be the lucky one."

"We'll just have to see where the garter lands…" Jem looked over at Jay. "Ready, brother-in-law?" Jay smiled and nodded his head. He looked over the group of men and turned his back toward them.

"One! Two! Three!" Jay tossed the garter over his shoulder.

"There it goes, and where it will land…" The garter sailed through the air toward the edge of the area where the men were standing. Sam, who had been in the group but was standing closer to the outer edges, reached out and caught it before it landed on the floor. He smiled as he whirled it in a circle around his finger and walked forward. Jay gave him a fist bump and smirked.

"The bouquet and garter have both been thrown and caught. Now, following tradition, Baleigh, have a seat. Sam, come over here." Jem pointed to where he needed him. Baleigh pasted a smile on her face to hide her nervousness and looked anywhere other than at Sam. She knew what his hands felt like on her body. She just hoped she could keep it together while he slid the garter up her leg.

Who the hell started this tradition anyway!? she wondered. Clearly, it was someone who was a shit-stirrer of the highest order. Yeah, that was it, and things were getting messier by the minute because her friends were doing the stirring. She was pretty sure they somehow arranged this scenario. She loved them, but they had to know, that even with all the love, happiness, and drinks flowing around today, there was no way this would end well.

Sam snuck a look over at a very pissed-off Kacey standing next to the evil twins who were both frowning as he walked over to stand in front of Baleigh, who'd just sat down. Jay's dad gave him a sympathetic glance and a thumbs-up. Seems he too knew the outcome of what was about to happen. Jesse had a big smile on his face as he moved to get into position to take more pictures. *Fuck it*, Sam thought. He'd been dancing around this issue long enough. There was no way he was going to hurt Baleigh again just to please someone he no longer wanted to be with.

He kneeled in front of her and paused for a moment. She looked at him questioningly. He smiled. "It'll be okay," he mouthed. She returned his smile with one of her own. He held up the garter, and she raised the hem of her dress slightly and moved her foot towards him so he could remove the bronze-colored, jeweled pump and guide the garter up her leg. She felt a jolt when he touched her. Judging from his quick intake of breath, Sam must have felt it, too. He maintained eye contact with her as his hands slid up along with the garter, which took her from nervous to hot, bothered, and wet. His eyes were filled with lust as he continued to gaze at her. She was grateful that no one could see his hands as they made their way up her leg. She hoped he'd stop soon. She was pretty sure she wouldn't be able to contain the moan that was threatening to escape her lips. Sam apparently noticed, because he squeezed her thigh and smirked as he removed his hands and stood up.

Jem cleared his throat. "Well, damn. Lisa and Jay," he looked over at the newlyweds, "it looks like y'all have a long and happy life ahead. How about a round of applause for the happy couple?" He looked over at Sam and Baleigh as he spoke. Lisa and Jay gave them both a hug. "DJ, let's keep this celebration going! Come on everybody, to the dance floor!" Jem walked toward the DJ and handed him the microphone. He grabbed Rich's hand and joined the other guests who were doing the first steps of the Cha Cha Slide.

Lisa grabbed Baleigh's hand and pulled her toward the doors leading to the outside area. They joined Eden and Nick who were standing near the bar. "Two bourbons please," Lisa told the bartender, "and two waters."

The bartender fixed the water first and handed them to her. "Congratulations," she said as Lisa took the glasses from her.

"Thank you." Lisa smiled and handed one of the glasses to Baleigh. "Girl, you look like you need this. I thought you and Sam were about to set the damn floor on fire."

"I have no idea what you're talking about," Baleigh mumbled as she raised her glass to drink.

"Don't act like you don't know what I'm talking about, Bibi." Lisa looked at her pointedly.

"Yeah, don't act like you don't know." Nick chuckled. "I felt it, and I was on the other side of the room."

"I didn't think tall, dark, and brooding had it in him. I told Nick I've been seeing a whole other side of Sam since we've been here," Eden added.

Baleigh drank the ice water and tried to avoid making eye contact with any of them. They were right, but she wasn't going to admit it. She set the empty glass on a nearby table and accepted the glass of bourbon from Lisa.

"I have a feeling that things are about to get all kinds of crazy, so I think I'll finish this and go find Jay. I kinda want to stick around and see how this all ends, but I *really* want to get the honeymoon started." She touched her glass to the others and tossed back her drink. She hugged Nick and Eden and thanked them again for being part of their special day. When she hugged Baleigh she whispered, "Thank you. This would never have happened without you. I wish you and Sam the best. Love you."

"Thanks," Baleigh said as she returned the hug. "Love you, too."

Lisa walked off to find Jay. Baleigh turned to look at Nick and Eden. "You two mind if I hang out with you for a bit?"

"No, not at all," Nick said as he walked over to Baleigh and put his arm around her shoulders. His other arm was wrapped around Eden's waist. "Let's have one more drink, and then let's burn up— I mean, hit the dance floor." Eden shot him a look and smacked him on the chest, and they all laughed.

Jay laughed as he stood with Sam and his father. He looked at Sam and was about to speak but started laughing again. His father was laughing along with him. "Man," he said as he sobered up, "you got some serious explaining to do. Your woman is over there looking like she's ready to commit murder, and Mom and Aunt Dahlia look like they want to help her."

"I agree." Jacob Sr. added. "Those are some *angry* women. You might want to consider going into the witness protection program, Sam." He grimaced, then started laughing again.

"Yeah, I probably should have thought more about the potential consequences of my actions."

"You should have, son, but I don't blame you. Baleigh seems like a good woman."

"Well Pops, in his defense, they do have history."

"They do?"

"Yeah. They met a while back. Dumbass over here was too scared to move forward with her. He hadn't seen her since then until he picked her up at the airport."

"Sam, I'm disappointed in you. In what universe do you let a woman like that get away?"

"I know. Don't think I haven't called myself all kinds of a fool over the years. But I'm done with that. I have an opportunity to be with her, and I'm taking it. I was just hoping to be able to talk with Kacey after the reception, but *some* people have other ideas." He looked at Jay.

"I'm not sorry. I'm sure it didn't escape your attention that most of the men, and a few of the women, have been eyeing Baleigh like a snack. I love you two, but clearly, you both needed a little help. Now, I see my bride headed this way, so I'm gonna go grab her and disappear. Pops, Sam, thanks for everything. Love you both." He hugged both men and went to Lisa who smiled and blew kisses in their direction before turning away as she walked out with Jay.

"I think I'll leave you to your thoughts. I'm going to go see what my wife is up to." Jacob Sr. patted Sam on the back as he left. Sam turned to scan the room. He saw Baleigh on the deck with Nick and Eden. Nick saw him and motioned his head toward Baleigh and smiled. Sam smiled back and continued to look over the room in search of Kacey. He spotted her coming out of the ladies' room and made his way over to her.

Kacey looked at him as he approached. She seemed calm. "Hey, Kace."

"I'm sorry, are you talking to me?" *No, not calm,* he thought. *Angry. Very angry.*

"Yes, I am. Can we go somewhere and talk?"

"Why should I go anywhere with you?" she asked angrily.

"Please, Kace." She was silent. He took her silence for a yes and grabbed her elbow to lead her out of the room to one of the other outdoor deck areas. He took her over to the chairs near the heat lamps and motioned for her to sit down.

"What's going on with you, Sam? You've been acting different ever since we got here," she started.

"That's not true."

"Yes, it is!" Her voice rose. "Your friends don't like me, and they're intent on breaking us up. They've been doing everything they can to keep you busy so we can't spend time together. And don't let me get started on that maid of honor. Don't think I don't know she's been hitting on you." Kacey was getting louder with each word that came out of her mouth.

"Listen, Kacey. We both came here to attend the wedding of my best friend. You knew I was in the wedding party. And my friends aren't like that." *A lie*, he thought, based on their actions a few minutes ago. "And leave Baleigh out of this," he added.

"Why should I leave her out of this? I've put too much time and effort into this relationship to let some random bitch tear us apart!" she yelled the last.

"Okay, first of all, you need to lower your voice. Second, you will not refer to Baleigh as *some random bitch*." His voice was calm, but the look she saw in his eyes made her nervous. He'd never looked at her like that before.

"Oh yeah?" she challenged. "What are you going to do if I don't?" Kacey knew she was poking the bear, but she wasn't willing to let Sam go. He wasn't thinking straight. She was pretty sure his friends were influencing his behavior. She would change that once they got back home. Sam continued to look at her. He shook his head.

"I can't do this."

"Do what?"

"Us. This. I can't do this! Look, Kace, you know things haven't been going well for us for a while now. So much so, that you were thinking about not coming to this wedding, and I was honestly hoping you wouldn't. I wanted some time away from you because I was thinking about ending things. But you decided to come, and here we are. I was going to wait to do this, but I can't. I'm done. It's over between us. I'm going to go to the front desk and order a car to take you to the airport tomorrow, then I'm going to the room and getting my shit. I hope you have a good life." He walked away from her.

"Sam, come back here! I'm not done talking to you! This is not over!" Kacey yelled, not caring who heard her. He kept walking. She watched him until he disappeared from her line of sight.

Baleigh and Eden were laughing at Nick as he told a story about the three of them as boys when Eden saw Kacey coming towards her. "Uh-oh," Eden said. "Baby, we got trouble." She nudged Nick who looked over his shoulder and rolled his eyes.

"Oh shit." He sighed. "Hey, Kacey, enjoying the reception?"

"What do you care?!" She glared at him.

"Guess not." Nick shrugged his shoulders.

"Baleigh, I don't know what it is you think you're doing, but you need to stop! I've had enough of you and your desperation. Sam is never going to be yours, so you need to leave him alone. And by leaving him alone, I mean I don't want to see you anywhere near him. He is *mine*. You must live in an alternate reality if you think you ever had a chance with him. There is no way a bitch like you could have a man like him!"

"Kacey, if anyone around here is desperate, it's you. I have nothing to do with whatever is, or was, between you and Sam. You must have lost your damn mind thinking you can come over here and talk to me like this. This is a wedding reception. It's not the time for you and your issues. Oh, and call me a bitch one more time, and watch what happens." Baleigh stepped closer to Kacey as she spoke the last. She hadn't intended to cause a rift between Kacey and Sam, but they'd been having problems long before she arrived here in Fallston. She knew the pain of a broken heart, and on some level, she understood Kacey's anger, but the heart wants what the heart wants. Looks like Sam had come through on his promise to her. Despite this drama with Kacey, she wasn't walking away from him.

Jacob Sr. followed by the evil twins came over to where they stood. "What in the world is going on here?" He looked at both women.

"I'll tell you what's going on! This b—" Kacey started.

"Oh, you thought I was playing?" Baleigh asked, taking a step closer to her. "Go ahead and call me out my name one more time."

Nick stepped between the two women, and Jacob Sr. grabbed Kacey's arm and gently pulled her over to where his wife and sister-in-law were standing. Eden wrapped her arm around Baleigh's shoulder, turning her towards the door to walk back inside.

Kacey was crying and fully engaged in playing the victim as Iris and Dahlia consoled her. Iris looked at Baleigh as she hugged Kacey.

"She should be ashamed of herself," Dahlia said, as she too glared at Baleigh. "It'll be okay. He deserves everything he gets if this is how he treats you. Don't lower yourself to her level."

Baleigh heard her as she walked past. She hated it had come to this. The way Kacey and the twins were carrying on, Baleigh alternated between wanting to cuss them out or slap the shit out of the three of them. But it was her best friend's wedding, she reminded herself, so she kept walking with Eden.

"Are you alright?" Eden looked closely at her.

"I'm fine. Since the reception is about over, I think I'm going to go upstairs and change shoes so I can come back down to talk to the hospitality manager and grab Lisa's stuff."

"Need any help?"

"No, I got it. But thanks anyway."

"Why don't you take your time coming back down. I'm sure more people will have cleared out by then." She nodded her head in the direction they'd come from.

"I think I will. Are you heading up?"

"Yeah, I'm gonna get Nick. You'll be at brunch tomorrow?

"Yes. See you then."

Eden gave her a hug. "I'm happy for you and Sam, good night."

Chapter 29

Baleigh entered her room, took off the shoes she'd worn for the wedding, and sat on the couch. It had been a long day, and the confrontation with Kacey had left her feeling emotionally drained. She knew she needed to get back downstairs, but what she wanted was to lay down on the bed and sleep. She got up to get the sneakers she planned to put on when she heard a knock. She had no idea who it could be, but she hoped it wasn't Kacey. Baleigh had had enough interaction with that woman to last a lifetime. She looked through the peephole and took a step back. She inhaled deeply to steady her breathing before she opened the door. There stood Sam with his suitcase and camera bag.

"Hey," Baleigh called, leaning against the door jamb.

"I hope you don't mind. I need a place to stay tonight. I would have gone to Jesse's room, but I think he may have company, and I'd hate to be a third wheel."

"We can't have you cramping Jesse's style now, can we?" Baleigh smiled and opened the door wider, stepping aside.

"No," he said as he stopped in front of her. "We cannot."

She closed the door, only to find Sam standing directly in front of her. He put his hands on the door, caging her in. He looked at her the same way he'd done earlier when he put the garter on her. She looked down. She suddenly felt a little shy. Sam removed one of his hands from the door, placed it under her chin, and gently lifted it.

"It's okay, Baleigh. I'm a little nervous, too, but we're doing this." He leaned forward and gently kissed her. "I heard about what happened between you and Kacey. I'm sorry. Are you okay?" he asked before he again brushed his lips against hers, coaxing her to lean in. This was not a sweet gentle kiss, but one that spoke of promise and erased any doubts she'd been harboring. When she felt Sam move closer and press his big body into hers, she broke away from the kiss.

"I hate to stop now, but I have to get back downstairs. I need to grab Lisa's stuff and speak with the hospitality manager before they start cleaning up."

Sam rested his forehead on Baleigh's. "Okay, but you owe me. And I am going to enjoy making you pay. You want me to go down with you?"

"No, you don't have to. It won't take long."

"Let me rephrase that. I said that as a question when it wasn't. I'm going downstairs with you."

"Well…" She smiled at his not-so-subtle demand. "When you put it that way, I guess you are." She moved away from Sam to get her shoes. Once she had them on, she grabbed her room key and walked over to Sam who had been standing near the door watching her. He opened it, and she preceded him into the hall.

He grabbed her hand and pulled her close as they walked to the elevator. Once inside, he pressed the button for the bottom floor and had her up against the wall all in a manner of seconds before his mouth was on hers again. When the elevator chimed their arrival, he stepped away and faced forward. Unfortunately, when the door opened, there stood Kacey with Dahlia, Jay's aunt. Both women were giving her death glares. Baleigh was tired and had had enough of Kacey's yelling and crying. She was done with Jay's aunt as well. Baleigh was all for respecting her elders, but after the way she'd been treated by her and Jay's mother, she'd reached her limit. She walked past Sam to exit the elevator, ignoring them.

"Bitch," Kacey hissed.

"Shut it, Kace. I won't tell you again." Sam looked at Kacey and Dahlia. "I suggest you continue on to your room and pack for your flight tomorrow. Don't let me hear you call Baleigh another name or say anything else about her, for that matter. You won't like what happens if I do." He grabbed Baleigh's hand, moving on.

Baleigh smiled as she walked beside Sam. He'd kept his promise to her. Yes, it didn't go quite the way they'd expected, but nevertheless, he did. She felt her stomach flutter as she thought about what that would mean for her and Sam going forward. Hearing him sticking up for her and being a man of his word had pushed her over the edge. She was in love with Sam McKinney. She was still scared, but she was fully ready to commit to whatever the future held for them.

Baleigh gathered Lisa's stole, which had somehow found its way to the dance floor and collected the remaining gifts and card box from the table that had been set up along the wall. She asked Sam to check the area by the wedding party's table as she spoke to the hospitality manager. Once done, she and Sam headed back up to her room.

"I love Lisa and Jay, but I'm glad this is over. I am exhausted," Baleigh said as she walked into the room and sat down.

"Same here. But I wouldn't have missed it for the world." She was sure the look in Sam's eyes matched her own. She hated the drama, but she would have gone through it again if it meant she would have the same outcome.

"I'm going to take a shower," she announced, going to the closet to remove her dress and grab her robe.

"Care for some company?" Sam asked. "We could save water if we do it together." Sam grinned wickedly at her.

"Sure."

Sam stepped out of his shoes, then rose and walked toward the bed, pulling his shirt from his pants and unbuttoning it. He took off the rest of his clothes and laid them on the chair near the bed. He grabbed his toiletry kit from his suitcase and followed her into the bathroom.

Sam got in the shower stall, turned on the water, and adjusted the temperature. Baleigh put her shower cap on before following him in. Sam looked at the bottles lined up on the built-in shelf and grabbed the shower gel. He flipped the cap open and squeezed some into a hand towel and began to rub it over Baleigh's body. It had been a long and emotionally exhausting day for her. He wanted to help her relax in any way he could. It was a struggle because what he wanted to do was be balls deep inside of her, giving her pleasure as she screamed his name. He'd give her time to rest, but after that, all bets were off.

Stepping out of the shower, Sam wrapped a towel around his waist, and grabbed one of the bath sheets from the towel warmer. He reached for Baleigh and began to towel her dry. When he was finished, he held her robe open and sent her into the bedroom. He quickly dried himself off and joined Baleigh, who could barely keep her eyes open once she stepped out of the shower. He was sure she was feeling the events of the day in a big way. He found Baleigh sitting on the bed with her back to him, putting lotion on her body.

"Let me do that." Sam took the bottle and gently rubbed lotion all over her body. His hands hypnotically lulled her senses. She alternated between moaning in appreciation and yawning. Sam chuckled. After he was done, he pulled back the covers on the bed.

She yawned again and lay down. Sam turned off the lights from the switch next to the bed, undid the towel, letting it fall to the floor, and climbed between the sheets. He pulled her close, and whispered, "Go to sleep, babe. It's been a long day." He kissed her forehead and drew her closer, so her head rested on his chest.

The last thing Baleigh remembered before falling asleep was snuggling up to his warm, hard body, feeling safe and content.

A few hours later, Baleigh woke up to Sam's head between her legs and his mouth on her wet pussy. He sucked on her clit as he moved his fingers in and out of her core. She could feel the stubble on his jaw rubbing on the sensitive skin of her inner thighs. Her breathing became faster, and she felt an orgasm building. She opened her mouth to call his name, but what came out was a whimper. The whimpers grew louder as she closed her eyes, feeling tears escape as her orgasm plowed into her. Sam alternately licked and sucked and pressed down on her thighs to keep her from moving away from him. He was relentless until she came apart again. Baleigh was breathless as she opened her eyes and saw Sam watching her. She watched him as his tongue licked the fingers he'd used to bring her pleasure, just as he'd done the first time they made love. And just like the first time, she became even more aroused and wanted more.

Baleigh was sleeping with her back pressed up against Sam's chest. She woke up this time to the feel of Sam's hands on her body and his lips on the back of her neck. "Mmmm," she said as his lips moved over a particularly sensitive spot just below her ear.

"Good morning," he said, his voice thick with sleep.

"Good morning," she replied. She could feel a sleepy smile forming on her lips as he continued to touch her.

"Sleep well? Feeling rested?"

"Yes, very much so."

"Good, because it's eleven o'clock. Aren't you supposed to be somewhere at noon?" he asked as his hands stroked the curve of her hip. Baleigh stayed where she was for a few seconds more as Sam's words registered. She quickly sat up.

"Oh, my goodness! We're going to be late!" She tried to get out of bed, but Sam pulled her back.

"Wait a minute. How about a proper good morning before you get up?"

"A proper good morning?"

"Yes. You know, the one where I make you feel good and you thank God for me *and* this new day?" He turned her around so that she was on her back. She started to speak, but Sam covered her mouth with his while his hands moved down to her breast and squeezed her nipples. Whatever she'd been about to say had quickly been lost in the sensation. "Don't worry," he said as his lips moved along her jaw to her neck. "We won't be *too* late."

Chapter 30

With the bulk of their families and wedding guests having early morning departures from the inn back to Denver, the bride and groom wanted to have a "thank you" brunch for their wedding party before they left for their honeymoon later that evening. Sam and Baleigh were thirty minutes late arriving at the Beaver and Bear Café in Fallston. The four of them, Lisa, Jay, Nick, and Eden, were sipping mimosas and Bloody Marys when they were shown to their table.

"Hey, you two. It's about time you showed up. After Nick told us what happened, I thought we were going to have to send out a search party." Jay laughed as Sam pulled out a chair for Baleigh.

"Sorry we're late. It's Baleigh's fault. She had a little problem getting out of bed this morning." Sam smirked. Baleigh felt her face grow warm, and with the lighting in the café, she was pretty sure they could all see her blushing.

"Is that right? And you, being the gentleman that you are, you gave her some d—I mean assistance to get her going?" Eden snickered. The whole table burst out laughing at that.

"Something like that."

Their waitress came over and took their drink orders, told them about the specials, and gave them menus. The conversation continued with ease among the couples as they talked about the wedding. When the waiter returned with Sam and Baleigh's drinks and refills for the others, Jay tapped his spoon against his glass.

"In what seems to be a marathon of toasts over these last few days, I'd like to propose one more. Lisa and I want to thank you again. You made our wedding adventure one to remember. The best man and the maid of honor getting stranded at the bottom of the mountain, the sleigh ride, the photo shoot, sneaking in the new vows during the ceremony, that *scandalous* bouquet and garter incident... And, lest we forget, the big dramatic fight scene that occurs at every wedding. I would have loved to have seen that, by the way, but I was busy welcoming Lisa to the family." Everyone laughed. "But seriously, we love you, and we truly thank you. If we had to do it all over again, we wouldn't change a thing. Here's to good friends and good times," he finished, raising his glass as he looked around the table.

The conversation picked back up around the table as they ate. "What I want to know," Nick looked at Sam and Baleigh, "is how you two managed to not run into each other before now."

"Well, whenever Lisa and Jay were in my area, it was just the two of them. It seems like Sam was always out of town whenever I came for a visit. I was on a last-minute work trip out of the country for the engagement party. I'm sure if I would have been able to attend, we would have met up there. But it is kind of odd though."

"I'm glad it worked out this way," Lisa told the table. "If it hadn't, I don't think things would be the way they are now. I mean, I remember Bibi telling me about meeting someone a while back, but I never would have guessed it would be someone I knew. And if it was, and I say this from a place of love, Sam wouldn't have been the first person to come to mind. The man she described was more like the Sam we see now, not the one we knew then."

"I know, right?" Eden added. "I'm only partially joking when I call you tall, dark, and brooding, but that description fits you perfectly. I like Baleigh, so don't eff this up!" Another round of laughter rang out around the table.

Still laughing, Sam said, "Tell us how you truly feel, Eden." He looked around the table. "I'm glad to be with Baleigh. We don't know where we'll end up, but we're looking forward to finding out."

"Isn't that why you two were late getting here?" This came from Nick and was met with more laughter as they ate and drank and just enjoyed each other's company. A few times during brunch, Sam grabbed Baleigh's hand and squeezed it as if to remind her of what he'd told her last night. This was really happening, and she couldn't be happier.

Later, they all rode back to the inn together and said their goodbyes in the lobby as the couples went their separate ways. Lisa and Jay were leaving later that evening for Spain. Eden and Nick were going back home in the morning. Sam was leaving the next day as well. He and Jesse were planning to go over the pictures for the wedding so they could have the proofs ready for Lisa and Jay when they returned. When Sam and Baleigh arrived back in their room, Sam asked her when she was heading back.

"I'm scheduled to fly out tomorrow afternoon."

"Could I interest you in changing your plans?"

"Maybe. What'd you have in mind?"

"I need to meet with Jesse about the wedding photos and to help him get his gear together, but if you could spare a few days and come home with me, I'd love to spend some time with you."

"I can. I wasn't looking forward to leaving," she confessed. "I would love to spend some more time with you as well."

"Good. Let's get online and get your flight changed."

"Why don't you go find Jesse? I can take care of that while you're gone."

"You sure?"

"Yeah."

"Okay, but you're going to have to give me a little something before I leave." He waggled his eyebrows as he backed her up against the wall. She giggled as he kissed the breath out of her. When he moved away, she stumbled a little.

"Hurry back."

Sam went to Jesse's room. He'd texted him earlier to remind him about brunch. Jesse responded by telling him he was in town, but he'd overslept. By the time he got back to the inn to shower and change, they'd probably be done. He said he'd catch up with Lisa and Jay before they left. Sam told him he'd let them know and that he'd meet Jesse after brunch to help him get his gear organized and packed.

Jesse answered his knock. He looked bleary-eyed, a little hungover, and based on his wet hair, recently showered. "Hey, son. How are you feeling? You look a little tired."

"I *am* tired. I went to a party last night with Rachel after the reception. She's the waitress I met earlier."

"Must have been some party."

"It was." Jesse smiled as if remembering the events of the night before.

"I hope you partied responsibly." Sam looked meaningfully at Jesse.

Jesse smirked. "I hope you did, too."

"Smart ass."

"So, I heard there was a fight between Miss Kacy and Miss Baleigh last night. What happened?"

"You were there when I put the garter on Baleigh, so you probably have an idea about how things went from there."

"Yeah, for old folk, you two sure lit things up." Jesse laughed.

"I'd planned to speak with Kacey after the reception, to let her know that I wanted to break it off, but that plan went by the wayside. I found Kacey and talked with her afterward. She wasn't happy, and she was not shy about letting me or anyone in the vicinity know how she felt. I tried to reason with her to no avail, so I said, "fuck it," and ended things right there. I hated doing it that way, but the more I listened to her screeching, the more I realized I'd made the right choice."

"So, what you're saying is Miss Kacey didn't go quietly into the night."

"Nope. And after I left her, she went and found Baleigh. That didn't go too well for her either."

"I can't believe I missed all that. I should have stuck around a little longer."

"I'm glad you didn't. It's not something a father wants his son to see. It wasn't my finest hour."

"What about Miss Baleigh?"

"What about her? My feelings haven't changed. Hell, after giving her that garter, they've intensified."

"Okay. TMI."

"Hey, I'm just being honest. You need to recognize that your father still has it going on."

"Yes, you do. You caught the eye of more than a few women at the wedding—young and old."

"Like I said, I still got it." Sam grinned.

"Whatever. But I'm glad about you and Miss Baleigh though."

"I'm glad you said that. She's going to be coming home with us for a few days."

"A few days with you, you mean. I'm supposed to go visit Nana and Pop when I get back. I'll be gone until the following week."

"I forgot about that."

"Yup. You'll have the house to yourself. I hope you behave and don't do anything I wouldn't do." Jesse laughed.

"Okay, Mr. Funny Man. Let's get this gear organized and ready to go. We need to get up early in case the road conditions change. Once was enough, and I don't want to take that chance."

"It couldn't have been that bad. At least you had Miss Baleigh to keep you company. All we had was Uncle Jay's mom, aunt, and your mean ex-girlfriend."

"Aww, come on, she wasn't that bad."

"Yes, she was. In the few years you were together, you only saw the side of her she wanted you to see. If you hadn't had the good luck to get stranded in Bennett, you probably wouldn't have been aware of her cracks. And I do mean cracks and *not* quirks. Now that I think about it, I am surprised she was able to hide her true personality from you for so long."

"Well, whatever the case, I can't help thinking I dodged a bullet. I can't even fathom what my life would've been like if I stayed with her. I am glad that door has closed."

Chapter 31

Déjà vu. Yup, that's exactly what this is, Baleigh thought as they pulled up in front of Sam's house. Five years ago, she was in an SUV next to Sam with Jesse in the back seat. The only difference now was they were all older, and while the SUV was the same make, it was a newer model. Sam had parked at the airport, so after landing they loaded up and left the lot. She was deep in thought during the drive from the airport. She was excited about being with Sam but still remembered the pain she felt at their parting. She'd barely dated afterward, partially because she was scared to open herself up again, and if she were honest with herself, she was still thinking about the what ifs with Sam. She still didn't know how she'd fallen so quickly and so hard for someone she barely knew. Until she met Sam, she'd never believed in love at first sight. In fact, she'd been a skeptic about love. It seemed to be good for everyone else but her. She'd be lying if she said she wasn't just the teeniest bit jealous when Lisa told her about her and Jay's engagement. She was genuinely happy for them, but she was lonely and had been for a long time.

Now she had a second chance with a man she'd longed for, for a long time. Love had a funny way of taking over one's best intentions. She wouldn't have been able to say no to Sam if she tried. And she had tried…but not very hard. Now she was here, wondering if she'd made the right choice. She hated the lingering fear that came with this feeling of déjà vu. She didn't know if she could survive another broken heart.

Sam got out of the truck, walked around to the passenger side, and opened Baleigh's door. "I'll open the door and turn off the alarm," he told her as they made their way to the front door. "Make yourself comfortable while Jesse and I bring everything in."

"Okay, thanks. Can you remind me where the bathroom is?"

"Sure. It's right here." He pointed to the hallway, just off from the kitchen.

"I'll be right back."

When Sam went back outside, he saw that Jesse had gotten most of the luggage out of the truck and had put it on the porch. He picked up Baleigh's suitcases and carry-on bag and went back inside. He put them in his bedroom at the back of the house. He went back out and grabbed his suitcase and saw that Jesse had placed the photography gear in the foyer and was taking his luggage to the guest house out back where he lived. He'd moved in a couple of months ago after his mother and her husband relocated back to her husband's hometown to take care of his aging parents. Jesse, who was finishing up his last year of college, had been planning on getting an apartment when Sam offered up the guest house.

Jesse had been accompanying him on some of his work assignments when his schedule allowed and was excited to move into the guest house next to Sam's studio, which was also on the property. Jessie had learned a lot about photography from him and enjoyed it to the point where it became more than just a hobby. And like Sam, he also had a talent for it. As for Sam, he enjoyed the time he spent with Jesse and was more than pleased about their shared passion for photography.

Baleigh was looking out the kitchen window at the small garden plot when Sam came up behind her. His warm breath and the touch of his lips caused her breathing to quicken. "Hey, babe."

She turned, put her arms around his neck, and said, "Hey." She reached up and kissed him. He tightened his hold, walking her backward until he lifted her onto the counter. He spread her legs and stepped between them.

"I'm glad you're here," he murmured against her lips. He started to deepen the kiss when he heard the sound of a throat clearing.

"Sorry to interrupt," Jesse said happily.

"You don't sound sorry," Sam grumbled as he broke the kiss and sighed with his forehead against Baleigh's.

"No, really, I am. I just wanted to let you know that I'm going out."

"Okay. Have fun."

"I will. Bye, Miss Baleigh. Bye, Papa Sam. You two kids behave yourselves." Jesse snickered as he walked out the door.

"He's gone now. You can open your eyes." Sam chuckled.

"I can't believe he walked in here, and we didn't hear him."

"I heard him. Don't be too hard on yourself. After all, you *were* under the influence of my kiss."

"Whatever, man." She laughed.

"So, what do you want to do tonight? If you're not too tired, I want to take you out on a date." Sam nuzzled her neck as he spoke.

"A date?"

"Yes, a date. We haven't really been on one, and there's someplace I'd like to show you."

"Really?"

"Yes, really." He kissed her. "What do you say?"

"I say yes. Where are we going?"

"It's a surprise."

"Well, can you give me a hint, so I at least know what to wear?"

"Casual and comfortable. Something you can have fun in."

"That doesn't help."

"That's the only hint you're gonna get." He lifted her off the counter. "Better get moving." He smacked her on the ass as she walked away from him. She tried to hide the smile that was forming on her face but failed miserably.

An hour later, she checked her appearance in the mirror. She had on a pair of jeans, an off-the-shoulder fitted black sweater, and black ankle boots. Her hair was in a low ponytail, and she had on silver hoop earrings. She'd added silver rings on her fingers and a black embossed leather bracelet. She finished the look with light makeup and plum-colored, matte lipstick. She added a spray of perfume and grabbed her phone, her small purse, and her leather jacket. She hadn't originally planned on packing the weathered jacket when she was getting ready to fly out to Colorado, but now, she was glad she did. She took one last look and went to the front of the house where Sam was sitting on the couch, scrolling through his phone. He was wearing dark-wash jeans and an untucked hunter-green button-down that enhanced the color of his eyes. His hair was still damp from his shower. He looked up when she entered the room and smiled.

"Ready?" He walked toward her looking like the sexy, confident man he was. *Damn*. She nodded because even though she wanted to use her words, they refused to form. "Let's go, beautiful," he said holding the door open for her.

Her surprise turned out to be dinner at Buster's, a small family-owned restaurant that was one of the area's best-kept secrets. It was very popular with the locals and had been since it first opened in the early 1970s. The décor hadn't changed much since then either it seemed, as it still had that circa '70s look. The menu offered only what the chef was cooking that day, and the food was delicious. After dinner, they went to a bar called Curley's. It featured live music and was located in an older part of town. When they arrived, the band was getting set up to play. Judging by the crowd, it seemed to be a popular place. Sam grabbed her hand as they entered and led her to a table. A beautiful, tall, mocha-skinned waitress with a colorful headwrap came over and hugged Sam.

"Hey, Sam! Long time, no see. How've you been?" She smiled.

"Hi, Layla. I'm good. You?" he said, returning her hug.

"Same. Working hard, going to school. The usual." She looked at Baleigh with curiosity. "Sooo, you know I'm nosy and all. Who's your friend?"

"Layla, this is Baleigh." He raised Baleigh's hand to his lips and kissed it. "Baleigh, this is Layla. Her uncle owns this place."

"Nice to meet you, Layla," Baleigh greeted the waitress.

"Nice to meet you, too, Baleigh, and welcome to Curley's. I had to ask 'cause Sam has never brought anyone here. It's usually just him, Nick, and Jay. I see you, Sam." She laughed and winked at him. "What can I get you two to drink?"

"What would you like?" He looked at Baleigh.

"Whatever you're having is fine."

"We'll have two bourbons neat."

"Okay. Be back with your drinks."

"You come here often?" Baleigh asked.

"I do. I've been coming here for a long time. Curley and my father were friends. My father was a professional musician. He played bass and sang. He would often sit in with the house band."

"Is that so? Do you play?"

"Some, but I'm a much better photographer than a guitar player."

"Seems like that talented, creative gene runs strong in your bloodline."

"A little bit." He held his thumb and forefinger up with a little space between them to illustrate his point.

"Well, well, well. Layla told me you were here. She also told me you had a beautiful woman with you. I didn't believe her, so I had to come see for myself." A tall, handsome, older African American man with golden brown skin, a soul patch, and a sexy smile came up to the table. Sam got up laughing, and hugged him.

"Curley Anderson, this is Baleigh Emerson. Baleigh, this is Curley. He's the owner and namesake."

"Hi, Mr. Anderson."

"None of this Mr. Anderson stuff. Just Curley, sweetness," he said as he raised her hand to his lips. Baleigh blinked at him as she felt the warmth of his lips on her skin. Curley Anderson oozed charm, and it was potent.

"Cut that shit out." Sam smiled as he pulled Baleigh's hand away from Curley.

"Aww, Sam. I'm just welcoming her to my establishment." He chuckled. "It's nice to meet you, Baleigh."

"Likewise." She smiled back at him.

"How was the wedding, Sam? I hated to miss it."

"It was nice. Lisa was a beautiful bride."

"Lena is planning on having them over when they get back from their honeymoon so she can hear all about it."

"How is Miss Lena?"

"She's doing good. Based on the latest test results, she is officially in remission."

"That's great to hear. Please give her my love and tell her I'll be over to see her soon."

"I will. She'll be glad to see you. It's time to get the evening started. Baleigh, it was nice to meet you. I'll catch up with you two a little later." He patted Sam on the back and then walked to the stage where he welcomed everyone to the club and introduced the house band.

The house band played a mix consisting of blues, old-school R&B, and neo-soul. Curley sang a few songs with the band at the beginning of the set. His voice was as smooth as his swag, with a bit of smoke. "They're good. I'm guessing your dad must have been pretty good too, if he sat in with these guys." Baleigh leaned closer to Sam as she spoke.

"He was. They used to call him their *Scottish Soul Brother*. He said that's how he got my mom to go out with him." Sam's eyes softened as he mentioned his parents. "My mom was a nurse, they met when he went to visit a friend who was in the hospital. He asked her out, but she refused. A few weeks later, she came to Curley's with some friends. My dad was singing that night. Sometime during that evening, he made his way over to her table and asked her out again. That time, she said yes. She said his voice put a spell on her that night that she couldn't break."

"Like father, like son." Baleigh lifted her glass and took a drink. "I mean, you didn't sing to me or anything, but you definitely put a spell on me. I think I know how your mother may have felt." Sam got up from the table, took her hand, and led her to the dance floor.

"Let's dance." The band was playing a cover of Al Green's *Simply Beautiful*.

At that moment, in the middle of a crowded dance floor, everything around them slowed down and blurred except the emotions Baleigh felt as Sam held her close. They were a mix of joy and desire, a rightness she'd never felt. It was almost overwhelming. As the song ended, he leaned down and kissed her on the sensitive spot just below her ear. "Are you ready for your next surprise?"

"I am. I'm starting to like your surprises." She gave him a soft kiss on the lips. They walked back to the table, and he grabbed her jacket from the back of the chair.

"Let's go say bye to Curley."

The next surprise turned out to be the river walk where she and Sam had gone when they first met. They walked along the river path hand in hand. "I thought it would be nice to go back to the spot where after arguing and awkward conversation, we were finally able to connect. Or as I like to think of it, the time I got my head out of my ass and started to see you clearly," he confessed, making her laugh.

"I thought about this place a lot over the years. I wondered how you were and if you'd found happiness. I felt a little guilty though, hoping that you'd found what you'd been looking for but also hoping you were miserable."

"I was miserable. And I hated how things ended with us." He stopped, turned, and pulled her close. "I don't ever want to feel that way again." There, in the middle of the path, with the lights of the city as a backdrop and the sound of the water as it lapped gently against the bank, Sam kissed her. It wasn't just a simple kiss. It conveyed an apology for the past and a promise of a future. This was no gentle, sweet kiss. It was deep and binding. It made her body tingle as it sparked heat throughout her core. The kiss seemed endless.

Later when they returned to Sam's house, they shared a shower. Baleigh had never been all that into shower sex, but being in the large, steamy stall with Sam had her re-consider that opinion. It might have been the magic of the evening they'd just shared. It may have been the feel of his hands on her body or the feel of his body when she touched him. Whatever the reason, she lowered herself to her knees in front of Sam. She grabbed his cock and swirled her tongue over, across the tip, and underneath the head where it connected to the shaft before taking it into her mouth. Moving her head lower, she gently suckled his balls and began to hum. She felt him harden and began to lick his length before sliding her hand up and down in a circular motion.

Sam hadn't been expecting her actions, and his knees almost buckled when he felt the vibration of her humming on his balls. Her tongue felt like silk as it swirled over him. He opened his eyes and watched as she took more of his length. The warm wetness of her mouth and the way she sucked his cock felt almost as good as when he was balls deep inside of her. *Almost.* When she began to hum again, he quickly moved away from her, knowing if he didn't, he would cum. While he'd certainly been enjoying the moment, he wanted to be inside of her when he did. He took her hand and brought her to her feet. He turned her towards the wall, then bent her slightly and entered her from behind. She cried out with his first stroke. He wrapped an arm around her lower abdomen, and with his other hand, he played with her nipples, pinching, and squeezing them, enjoying the sexy sounds she made in response. He increased his pace, and her body matched his movements. Hearing her breathing intensify and feeling her pussy begin to tighten around his cock, his hand left her nipples, and he stretched his arm across her chest from shoulder to shoulder. He raised up slightly as she arched her back and began to moan loudly, her voice hoarse from their lovemaking. He quickly followed. When he slipped out of her and began to move away, she stumbled as her legs struggled to support her. He grinned and turned her around and kissed her soundly. He backed her up against the wall where he held her as he washed her body. By the time he finished, she was able to stand on her own. He then quickly washed and turned off the water.

Exiting the shower, he wrapped a towel around himself, then grabbed another towel and dried Baleigh. He lingered over the task, enjoying every minute of it. She, on the other hand, could barely keep her eyes open. Hanging the towel on the rack after he was done, he applied a sweet-smelling almond lotion she'd left on the counter earlier to her skin, then carried her to his bed where he joined her after drying himself off. Pulling the covers over their bodies, he kissed her softly and told her he loved her.

Baleigh contently lay in Sam's bed with her arms around him. She and Sam had made love many times, but tonight was different. This time, they connected on a whole other level, and she loved every minute of it. It had been so good; she could barely stand when he finished. He didn't say anything about her condition, but she did catch his sexy, lopsided grin a few times as he took care of her. He kissed her, then surprised her when he told her he loved her. She was almost asleep when she heard him say those three words. She did the only thing she could do after that; she told him she loved him too before drifting into a blissful sleep.

Chapter 32

The next day after breakfast, Sam and Jesse were in Sam's studio going over the wedding photos. After logging into work and checking her emails and the status of some projects she'd been working on, she decided to go shopping. She told Sam her plan, and he offered her the use of his truck. After finding a parking spot, she headed into Miller Street Plaza, an open-air shopping area that specialized in local arts and crafts. She lost track of time as she strolled through the various boutiques and pop-up shops. She purchased a pair of earrings, two scarves, and a jar of edible chocolate body paint. The latter, she couldn't wait to use on Sam. She was getting warm just thinking about spreading the decadent treat all over him and licking it off. She was caught up in her musings when her phone rang. She saw it was Sam.

"Hey, Sam."

"Hi."

"How's it going with the pictures from the wedding?"

"We just finished. I think Lisa and Jay will be pleased."

"Nice."

"Still shopping?"

"Yes, but I'm pretty much done and am about to head back."

"Okay. See you soon."

"Bye." Baleigh ended the call and walked back to the truck.

When she pulled up to Sam's house, he was sitting on the porch talking to Jesse and two older people. She grabbed her purchases, got out, and walked up the steps to join them. "Hi, babe." Sam stood up and kissed her on the lips.

"Hey, Miss Baleigh," Jesse greeted her.

"Baleigh, this is Erica and Jason Harris, Jesse's grandparents. Erica and Jason, this is Baleigh," Sam introduced her to the older couple.

"Hi, Baleigh. It's nice to meet you." Jason Harris held out his hand.

"It's nice to meet you, too, Mr. Harris, Mrs. Harris."

"Please," Mrs. Harris said, "call us Jason and Erica." She smiled. "Looks like you've been shopping."

"Yes, I decided to get a little retail therapy while these two were working on the wedding portfolio. I ended up at the Miller Street Plaza."

"I love that place. I always find such cute pieces, and they have good prices."

"They do. It was hard to leave."

"That's the way I feel when I go there." Both women laughed.

Jason cleared his throat. "Speaking of leaving, I hate to rush, but we need to get going." He looked at Baleigh. "We came by to pick up Jesse. He's going to spend some time with us old folks before school starts back," Jason joked. "Take care, and we hope you enjoy your visit."

Jesse gave Sam, then Baleigh, a hug. "I'm glad you're here," he said as he gave her a tight squeeze.

"Me, too," she responded. He picked up a duffle bag and his camera kit and followed his grandparents to their car. Sam put his arm around Baleigh as they watched them drive off.

"I have a question." Baleigh turned to Sam.

"Yes?"

"How would you like it if I cooked dinner for us?"

"I would first ask if you could cook. Then, depending on your answer, I would either say "I'd like that" or "Let me cook for you." So… can you… uh, cook?" His eyes held a teasing glint, and his lips twitched. Baleigh playfully narrowed her eyes at him.

"Yes, I can cook. It's been a long time since my food made anybody sick."

"Okay, I'm going to take a chance and say I like that idea."

"Then let's go to the market. I've seen your cupboards, and they're seriously lacking."

After some discussion on the way to the market, they decided on a menu of grilled salmon, risotto, and a salad. Sam grabbed a basket at the market entrance, and they made their way over to the produce section.

"You want to know the reason my cupboards are lacking?"

"You can't cook?"

"No."

"You don't know how to operate the stove?"

"No. What does that have to do with my poorly stocked pantry?"

"Nothing. I was just taking a guess."

"Well, sad to say, I'm not home very much, so I usually just order in or go out to grab a meal. Although, since Jesse moved in, I do try to cook a little more often when I'm home. I get him to help me because he needs to know how to do more than study, take pictures, and get spoiled by the women he dates."

"So, the ladies are after him, huh? Can't say that I blame them. He's a handsome young man, and he's really sweet."

"A chip off the old block." Sam bumped Baleigh's shoulder and laughed.

"Whatever, man." She laughed with him. They finished shopping and loaded the bags into the truck. Sam stopped at a wine shop on the way home and picked up wine to accompany the meal. "There's a specialty bakery across the lot. You want dessert?" he asked as he got in the car.

"No, what we have is fine." Baleigh smiled as she thought about the edible chocolate paint she'd purchased earlier that day.

"You sure?"

"I'm sure. Let's go, I'm hungry."

He started the truck. "Yes, let's get you fed. You're going to need your strength later on." He smirked and pulled out of the parking lot onto the street.

"Are you sure you know what you're doing?" Sam handed her a glass of wine as he looked over Baleigh's shoulder.

"Yes, I know what I'm doing." She continued to toast the rice as she took a sip from her wine glass. "You don't make risotto the same way you cook other rice. You toast it, then you add the broth, butter, then the parmesan cheese."

"Looks like a lot of work."

"It's not that much work. And speaking of work, is the grill ready?"

"Yup. Should I put the salmon on now or wait until that gets closer to being done?"

"We can wait a bit. But you can start the salad if you want, and I'll make the dressing."

"You're making the dressing from scratch?"

"I am. I always hate having a bunch of bottles of salad dressing in the refrigerator that I never seem to use more than once. When I make my own, I have just what I need. Wanna help?"

"Sure, tell me what to do."

She grabbed the fresh dill they'd purchased earlier and put them on the cutting board and slid it toward Sam.

"Chop these up, and when you're done, mix the dill with the olive oil, vinegar, garlic, oregano, salt, and pepper. When you're done with that, we'll make a sauce to go over the salmon." After listening to her go on, Sam could honestly say he was impressed.

"Maybe you *can* cook." Sam smiled at her.

"Oh, yeah. You can cook," he said later after they finished eating. "That was delicious. The only thing that would have made it better is if you would've been naked under an apron while you prepared it." He raised his eyebrows over the rim of his wine glass. "Just saying." Baleigh laughed. "Think about it. I could be sitting with my drink at the counter, watching you put together a meal. It would be like watching a sexy cooking show."

"Would you be naked, too?"

"No, but watching you would work up an appetite, which could enhance your kitchen experience." The heat in his eyes spoke of what that kitchen experience might be.

"Interesting. Maybe I'll go apron shopping tomorrow."

"Maybe I'll go with you." He wrapped his arms around her and gave her a quick kiss. "The food is put away, and the kitchen is clean. The sky is clear tonight. There's a full moon. Let's go sit on the back deck." She said yes to that. Sam grabbed a quilt, and they went out and snuggled together on one of the couches.

"This is nice, Sam."

"It is. I never thought I would see you again when I left your room five years ago. I'm glad I was wrong. I can't think of any place I'd rather be than right here with you," Sam whispered against her lips. He pulled her closer and let his tongue in her mouth say everything else he couldn't there under the light of the full moon. Baleigh felt like she was in a dream. They continued to talk and share kisses as they lounged together wrapped in the quilt. She'd never felt so relaxed and content. The feel of Sam's big, warm body soothed her. They both drifted off to sleep under the light of the moon and stars.

"Sam! What the hell is going on? Why haven't you returned my calls?" Baleigh raised up when she heard a woman's voice yelling. The angry voice was none other than Kacey's. What the hell was she doing there? Seems like they'd fallen asleep on the back deck and awakened to a nightmare.

"What are you doing here, Kacey? Better yet, how did you get in?" Sam asked angrily as he sat up on the couch.

"The side gate was unlocked. I came over to talk to you."

"Since it's unlocked, I recommend you take your ass out the same way you came in."

"You can't mean that. After all this time together, you're choosing her over me? Really, Sam? Is this who you want in your life?"

"Kace—"

"You might want to wait to hear me out before you say something you might have to take back, Sam."

"What are you talking about?"

"I'm talking about the fact that I'm late."

"You're what?" he asked.

"I'm late. As in, I might be pregnant, and you might become a father for the second time."

"And you think that would change things between us?"

"Yes. I know you missed out on Jesse's early years. This would give you a chance to experience them with our child."

"You don't even know if you're pregnant, and even if you were, it would still be over between us. I'd take care of my responsibilities as a father, but know this, Kace, that does not mean you and I would be getting back together. You need to leave."

"She needs to leave. I'm not going anywhere. We need to talk!" She pointed at Baleigh who'd gotten up from the couch.

Baleigh couldn't believe what she was hearing. Kacey was pregnant? She looked at both Sam and Kacey. Kacey was crying and seemed near hysterical as she yelled at Sam. Sam looked angry, but his voice was calm. "You need to leave now. Don't make me tell you again."

"Fine. I'll go. But this isn't over." She walked down the steps from the deck and walked around the side of the house to exit the gate she'd come in through.

"Sam, is this true? Is she pregnant?" Sam didn't answer. He ran his hands through his hair and let out a deep breath. "Did you hear me? I asked you a question."

"I heard you."

"Well, is she pregnant?"

"Maybe. I don't know." He turned from her.

"What does that mean?"

"It means I don't know. We were in a long-term relationship. She was on the pill, and I stopped using condoms. We were together for three years. This has never happened in all the time we were together."

"So, what are you going to do?"

"I don't know."

"You don't know?"

"No. I don't!" He raked his fingers through his hair again. "Look, I'm sorry. I didn't mean to yell at you. This is crazy." He stood in front of her and ran his hands gently up and down her arms. "Let's go inside. I'll make some coffee, and we can talk about this." He opened the door leading into the house. Baleigh walked in ahead of him.

"I want to take a shower first."

"Okay. I'll be in the kitchen when you're done."

As Baleigh stood under the warm shower spray, she thought about what had just happened. This was crazy. What if Kacey was pregnant? That would mean Kacey would always be in his life. What would that mean for them? Baleigh knew she could never come between him and his child. She also didn't think she wanted to handle having to deal with Kacey should things continue to progress between her and Sam. "Too many unknowns," she said to herself. "I can't consider a future with Sam as long as Kacey is in the picture." She made up her mind that she would go home. She loved Sam, but this was too much. So much for second chances. She sighed as tears began to flow and mingle with the shower spray. After coming to her decision, she got out of the shower, got dressed, and packed her things.

Sam was leaning against the counter with a coffee cup when she walked into the kitchen. His hair was wet, and he'd changed into a t-shirt and faded black joggers. He appeared to be in deep thought.

He looked up when he saw Baleigh walk in. She was dressed and had her phone in one hand and her purse in the other. "What's going on?"

"I'm going home."

"You're going home? Why?"

"I can't stay here right now. I need some space."

"What do you mean you need some space? I thought we agreed to give things a try."

"We did. And I want to, but I can't. I can't do this." She hated the way her voice trembled.

"Come on, Baleigh. This is something we can work through. This doesn't have to be an end for us. We're just getting started."

"I know. Maybe this was all too good to be true. If Kacey is pregnant, I know you'll be there for your child. She'll make every effort to get you back, and I wouldn't put it past her to use your child to do it. I just don't think I can do this. I'm sorry, Sam." She quickly wiped the tears that had slipped out as she spoke. Sam pulled her to him and wrapped his arms tightly around her.

"Baleigh, we can get through this. It's you I want to be with. If she's pregnant, I'll deal with it. I love you." Baleigh felt tears spill from her eyes and make their way down her face. Sam held her close. As the tears subsided, she pulled away.

"I love you, too. I'm sorry, Sam." She walked out of the kitchen. The Uber she'd ordered had arrived. She went to the bedroom to get her luggage. She looked at Sam one last time before she walked out the door. Her heart felt as if it had broken into pieces. She could feel the piercing of every single piece as she walked out the door.

What the fuck just happened?! Sam threw the coffee cup he'd set on the counter earlier against the wall. *How could she leave him?* He'd opened his heart to her, and she shattered it and walked away. He went over to the window and watched as she walked down the pathway to the waiting car. After she'd gotten into the car, she rolled down the window and looked back at the house. They both watched each other as the car pulled away from the curb. She said she couldn't do this. Well, neither could he. He was stupid enough to walk away from Baleigh five years ago and he wasn't about to walk away now. He'd let her have some time, but this wasn't over. Whatever the outcome with Kacey, one thing was clear: Baleigh was it for him. He didn't know how he was going to do it, but he was going to get her back.

An hour later, Sam had changed clothes and was pulling into the parking lot behind Nick's diner. He told himself he was going to grab breakfast, but he was lying. He needed to talk to his friend. Thankfully, the breakfast rush had ended, and now the diner was almost empty.

"Hi, Andrea. How are you?" he greeted the hostess as he walked in.

"Hi, Sam. I'm fine. You?"

"No complaints."

"Have a seat and I'll get you some coffee."

"Thanks." Sam took his usual seat at the counter.

"Hey, man! I'm surprised to see you here," Nick said from the other side of the counter. "What's up? Where's Baleigh?"

"Hey." Sam waited until Andrea poured his coffee and left before he continued. "You have a minute?"

Nick looked at Sam, alarmed at his demeanor and how flat his voice sounded. "Yeah, sure. Let's go back to my office." He refilled his coffee cup and led the way to the back of the diner.

"Are you okay?"

"No, I'm not. I've just had the morning from hell." Sam sat down. "Everything was fine until this morning when Kacey showed up."

"Damn, man."

"It gets better. She might be pregnant."

"Say what?"

"You heard me right. She said she was pregnant." Sam paused to take a drink from his cup. "Oh, yeah, and Baleigh left."

"What do you mean she left?"

"I mean she's gone. She went home."

"Wow. What are you going to do?"

"First, I'm going to get Kacey to a doctor and find out if she's pregnant. If she is, I'll be there for my child, but that's it. Next, I'm going to get my woman back. She said she would be able to handle me being a father, but she didn't think she could handle Kacey."

"I hate that for you, Sam. But knowing Kacey, I can understand how Baleigh might feel. I also know that you would make sure that Baleigh would be just as much a priority in your life as a child would be."

"I need to tell her that. I realize that now, but I couldn't see past her walking away."

"Whatever you need from me, just let me know."

"Thanks Nick."

Chapter 33

It had been two weeks since she'd left Sam. She was numb and was going through the motions of living. She'd been working remotely since she'd been back because she couldn't muster up the energy to leave home. She'd also stopped answering her phone. Sam had called her numerous times, but she couldn't bring herself to answer. Each call from him brought on a new bout of tears. She just couldn't make herself do it. She initially responded to a few of his texts, but those made her cry too, so she stopped. Lisa called, and she sent those calls to voicemail as well. She knew they had recently returned from their honeymoon, but she didn't have it in her to pretend interest as she listened to her friend talk about her trip. She lay in bed going back and forth with herself as to whether she should get up or stay where she was. Staying in bed was a compelling option. That way, she could keep the shutters closed and stay under the covers and cry herself back to sleep. And that's exactly what she did.

She heard her doorbell ring but chose to ignore it. It rang again, and then she heard knocking on the door. She really hoped whoever it was would go away. She pulled the covers more securely over her head and rolled over on her side. It was then that she heard Lisa's voice.

"Bibi, where are you? I know you're in here!" She heard the door to her bedroom open.

"My goodness, girl!" Lisa turned on the lamp next to the bed and walked over to the windows to open the shutters. She slid open the windows and sat on the side of the bed. "Hey, Bibi." She put her hand on Baleigh's shoulder.

"What are you doing here?"

"I heard what happened. You wouldn't answer my calls or text messages, so I came to see if you were okay."

Bibi rolled over to face Lisa. "I'm fine. You wasted a trip."

"No, you're not. We've been friends way too long for you to think you can get away with lying to me."

"Whatever, Lisa. Look, I don't want to be rude, but you should probably go. I'm not good company right now, and I don't want to disrupt your newlywed vibe."

"You're my best friend, and you're hurting. I don't care if you're not good company. I just need you to know that I'm here. I also need to tell you to get your ass out of this bed and take a shower."

"Did you not hear what I just said?"

"Yes, I heard you, but I'm not leaving. Get up and get dressed. When you finish, come downstairs, and I'll make breakfast."

Sam sat at his desk and booted up his computer. Jesse texted him earlier to tell him he'd finished uploading the remaining pictures from the wedding. He wasn't really in the mood to do so, knowing that Baleigh was probably in quite a few of them. Except for a few texts she'd responded to, he hadn't heard from her since she left his home two weeks ago. She wasn't taking his calls or replying to his texts or his voicemails. Sam knew he needed to put his hurt feelings aside and try and see things from her point of view, and then maybe he'd get somewhere.

Sighing, he accessed the folder. The pictures *were* from the wedding trip; however, these weren't of the wedding party. They were pictures Jesse had taken of Sam and Baleigh. Sam felt an ache in his chest as he viewed them. He had no idea Jesse had taken so many of the two of them. There was one of them in the sleigh, heads back laughing, one of them leaning into each other, and another of him reaching for her hand.

Finally, there was the reception. Jesse had snapped a picture of the two of them walking down the aisle at the end of the ceremony. Their smiles were as bright as the bride and groom. The next was of him, Baleigh, and Jesse. Sam smiled, thinking how they looked like a family. Jesse captured the introduction of the wedding party when Sam had spun Baleigh around. She'd smiled at him in surprise, laughing. The move had been spontaneous on his part, and he was glad he'd done it. The joy he saw on her face warmed his heart. The last picture was the "infamous" garter incident. He remembered every detail. Looking at the photograph, he could see what everyone had been teasing him about. It was *not* a PG scene, that's for sure.

Sam would give anything to have Baleigh with him at that moment. He missed her. He wanted to see her smile and hear her laughter. He wanted to hold her and feel her heartbeat. He wanted to hear her breathless moans as he made love to her. The ache in his chest intensified as he looked at the photos on the computer screen. Baleigh was it for him. He needed to find a way to get her back.

Chapter 34

It took angry words and multiple threats to finally get Kacey to the doctor to confirm her pregnancy. Sam suspected she'd been lying. He wanted confirmation either way so he could get on with his life. Now, here they were at the doctor's office for an ultrasound appointment. Sitting next to Kacey, all he could think about was Baleigh. These past two weeks had been hell. He missed her and it hurt to breathe. She'd taken his heart with her when she left.

"I think we should talk about how we're going to do this," Kacey said. "I was thinking that maybe we could look at moving in together. It would be easier on our child. I sent you some links to a couple of homes you might like. They're in good school districts and are only about an hour's drive from here. Did you look at them?"

"No. I didn't, and I'm not going to. I told you whether you were pregnant or not, there is no you and me. We're over. I will keep repeating what I've already told you until it sinks in," he said to her in a detached voice.

"You don't mean that. Look, we just hit a rough patch, all couples do at one time or another. With everything going on with the wedding, Baleigh was a distraction. We can get through this and get back to us."

It was as if she hadn't heard anything he'd been saying to her. Sam took a deep breath and was about to respond when the nurse called Kacey's name. Kacey got up and smiled.

"Come on, Sam."

"Hi, Kacey. How are you doing today?" the doctor greeted her.

"I'm doing fine, Dr. Rossman. This is my boyfriend, Sam McKinney." Kacey smiled at the doctor. Sam decided to let it slide.

"Hi, Dr. Rossman."

"Mr. McKinney." The doctor nodded. "Now, let's get started. Kacey, I know you said you've taken several pregnancy tests that have all had positive results."

"That's correct, doctor. I've also experienced things that make me think I might be pregnant."

"Such as?"

"Weight gain, breast tenderness, and I've been a lot more tired than normal."

"Okay. When was your last period?"

"About six weeks ago, and I've always had regular cycles."

"We'll do the ultrasound, and afterward, we can discuss what happens next."

"Sounds good."

"I'm guessing since Mr. McKinney is here, he's staying for the ultrasound also."

"Yes, I am," Sam said quickly.

"He is," Kacey confirmed.

"Marilyn, the nurse who's going to assist me, will come in and get you ready." Dr. Rossman left the room.

"You said your last period was six weeks ago, correct?" Dr. Rossman asked as she moved the transducer over Kacey's flat abdomen.

"Yes, six weeks ago."

"Hmmm…"

"Is anything wrong, doctor?"

"No. I'm going to take a few snapshots, and then we'll be done." She moved the transducer around and paused to take pictures.

"Okay, we're done. When you get dressed, meet me in my office next door please."

"Sure, Dr. Rossman." Kacey looked slightly worried. On her way to use the toilet, she wondered what the doctor had seen on her ultrasound. When she came back into the exam room, she found Sam watching her with a strange look on his face that she couldn't read. He said nothing as she got dressed. He held the door open for her to precede him into the doctor's office, and they both took a seat.

"Kacey, going over your lab results and the ultrasound, I have not found evidence of a pregnancy. The home tests you took gave you a false positive, which can sometimes happen." Dr. Rossman looked at Kacey sympathetically.

"Are you sure? Maybe it's too early for the ultrasound test."

"You said you were six weeks late for your cycle. At four and a half to five weeks, we would have been able to see the fetus. Normally at six weeks, we would have been able to have an even better picture, but there wasn't one. And as far as your labs go, the blood tests for pregnancy have a 99 percent accuracy rate. Those results were also negative. I'm sorry, Kacey. You're not pregnant."

Kacey started to cry. "That's not possible, doctor. I know my body. I felt the changes." Dr. Rossman pushed a box of tissues toward her.

"You may have very well felt changes. But the symptoms you described are also common with PMS. I'm sorry." She got up and walked around her desk, placed a hand on Kacey's shoulder, then left the office.

Sam didn't consider himself a religious man, but he gave a silent prayer of thanks when he heard the doctor say Kacey was not pregnant. He looked over at Kacey who continued to cry. He supposed he should be feeling something for her, after all, they'd been together for three years. But he didn't. The only thing he felt was relief. He stood from his seat and gave her two last words before walking out the door. "Goodbye, Kacey." And he was gone.

On the way to his truck, he texted Jay and Nick to meet him at their favorite sports bar. He smiled to himself. He was going to get that second chance with Baleigh after all. She'd been avoiding him, but it was time for that shit to stop. He was getting his woman back, and this time he wasn't letting her get away.

Chapter 35

Sam arrived in the parking lot of Eli's Sports Bar and saw Nick and Jay walking toward the entrance. Jay had not long returned from his honeymoon, and this was Sam's first time seeing him since he'd been back. "Hey, fellas!" he called to them as he got out of his truck. They did the bro-hug thing. "Welcome back, Jay."

"Thanks, although I could have happily stayed gone a little longer."

"I'm sure you could have."

"How are you doing, Sam?" Nick looked at him closely.

"I'm good. Let's go inside. First round is on me." Sam patted him on the back.

After being seated and placing their orders with the waitress, Nick asked Sam how the doctor's appointment went.

"It went great. I'm *not* the father because Kacey is *not* pregnant."

"What? Really?"

"She either got a false positive from the pregnancy tests she'd taken, or she was lying."

"I'm guessing she was lying." Nick looked at both men. "What? You don't think so? Not wanting to say anything bad about your mother, Jay, but this looks like the handiwork of the evil twins."

"No, I don't think they would encourage her to lie about something like that."

"I'm not so sure. But anyway, I'm glad she's not pregnant. What are you going to do now, Sam?"

"What do you think I'm going to do? I'm going to get Baleigh to take me back."

"That might be easier said than done," Jay told Sam.

"I don't expect it to be easy."

"I don't think you understand, Sam. Lisa went to see Bibi when she wouldn't return her phone calls. She was in bad shape when she arrived. She was sad, wouldn't leave the house, wouldn't even get out of bed. If Lisa hadn't had a key, I don't think Bibi would have let her in. Now she's angry. I'm going to say this one more time. After everything you've put her through, if you're not serious about her, you need to walk away. For good."

"I haven't known her long, but I agree with Jay," Nick added.

"I am serious. I know I hurt her. I never meant for that to happen. I love her, and I intend to get her back."

"Alright, Sam. But if she doesn't want you, that's it. *You move the hell on.*" Jay looked pointedly at him.

"What he said," Nick chimed in.

The waitress brought their drinks. Sam raised his glass. "Gentlemen, mark this day. A year from now, you'll be attending the wedding of myself and Ms. Baleigh Emerson." They clinked glasses and drank.

"You do realize you're going to have to work to get her back, right?" Jay set his glass on the table.

"I do. And I'm gonna need you two to help make that happen. Jay, when is Lisa coming back?"

"She'll be back at the end of the week."

"Nick, do you think I could rent out the diner for a few hours?"

"Sure. What did you have in mind?" Sam leaned in towards the two men and told them his plan.

Later that night, Jay told Lisa about Sam's plan to get Baleigh back. "Do you think it will work?"

"I don't know. She's pretty mad at him."

"Do you think you could at least get her to come here?"

"I'll try. Do you think Sam is seriously done with Kacey?"

"He said he was. I believe him."

"Okay. But I'm going to kick his ass if he hurts her again."

"I told him the same thing, but enough about them... I miss you."

"I miss you, too." They remained on the phone a little longer and said good night so Lisa could talk to Baleigh and start working to persuade her to go home with her at the end of the week.

Nick and Eden were getting ready for bed when he told her Sam's plan.

"I think he'll be able to pull it off." Nick placed his electric razor on the counter and ran his hand over his chin.

"He'd better. I like him with Baleigh. Tall, dark, and brooding's personality was getting darker by the day when he was with Kacey. Baleigh is good for him. I think I even saw him smile once with her." She laughed.

"That's not funny. You're talking about my brother."

"I know, but you know I'm right. He *is* better with her."

"You're right. But you know who's better than them?" Nick grabbed Eden.

"You better say *us* fool, or you're sleeping on the couch."

Nick smacked her ass and kissed her. "Us. Always."

Chapter 36

"I can't believe I let you talk me into this," Baleigh said to Lisa as she placed her suitcase in the overhead bin.

"Quit complaining. It'll be fun. You know I was never any good at organizing, and since my assistant quit, I've gotten worse. Why do you think Jem had to step in and help with the wedding plans?"

"Speaking of Jem, why didn't you call him to help?"

"He and Rich are out of town. Plus, I want you to help Jay organize his home office."

"Did you ask him? You know how he is about his stuff."

"I know, but you're a consultant. You help people position themselves to perform better. *And* you're good at it. When I first mentioned helping him, he took a hard pass. When I asked if he would let me do it if you were working with me, he agreed."

"Alright, well, once we get airborne let's start planning on how I can help you get your shit together."

"Thanks Bibi, I really do appreciate this." They spent the flight discussing options for Lisa and Jay to consider for their respective businesses.

Lisa waved at Jay as he pulled along the curb at the arrivals area of the airport. He'd been in the cell phone parking lot, and it hadn't taken him long to get there when she texted him to let him know they'd landed. He got out of the car and kissed Lisa.

"I'm glad you're back, baby, I missed you."

"Did you miss me, too?" Baleigh joked.

"Hey, Bibi! How's my girl!" He enveloped her in a hug. "Of course I missed you."

"I missed you too, Jay!" She laughed.

"Let's get your bags loaded so we can get moving."

"I hope you ladies are hungry." Jay looked over at Lisa in the passenger seat and the rearview mirror at Baleigh.

"We are." Baleigh replied. "Someone was running late today, and we not only missed breakfast, but we barely made our flight."

"I don't know what you're talking about. You're the one that overslept."

"Only because you took my phone off the charger. You know, the alarm doesn't work when the phone is dead."

"I know, but what was I supposed to do? I dropped my charging cord in the dishwater. I was going to need it to be fully charged for today. Besides, you were able to charge your phone on the plane. Now, back to your question, honey. Yes. We're hungry."

"That's good. Because we're going to Nick's for dinner. He has a new dinner menu he's trying out. Is that okay with you two?"

Baleigh started to feel a little uncomfortable. Nick was one of Sam's best friends. She hadn't known him long, and she wasn't sure how he'd be around her since she and Sam broke up. She didn't want to deal with any awkwardness.

"I don't know. Maybe, you can just drop me off and you guys go ahead."

"Come on, Bibi." Lisa looked back at her. "It'll be fun. Nick's cousin, Milos, is the chef. He's funny, and his food is amazing."

"If you're worried about running into Sam, don't be. He's on assignment and won't be back until tomorrow or so," Jay added. She said yes, even though she didn't want to go.

"Trust me. You'll be glad you did." Jay winked at her in the rearview mirror.

One of these days she was going to have to learn how to say no to the two of them. Leaning over to look at the passing scenery, she tried to get a handle on her emotions. Her heart was fragile. The thought of being around people who knew and loved the man that caused her condition made her both angry and sad. Angry because, like them, she loved him, and his lack of action in cleaning up his past had hurt her. Sad because she loved him, and he'd broken her heart. She just wanted to help her best friend and go home. The good memories of this city were buried under the heartache they had become. *It's going to take a lot to get through this evening,* she thought as she reached up to wipe away a tear before anyone noticed.

"Baleigh! How are you?" Nick greeted her with a hug. "It's good to see you!"

"I'm good. It's good to see you, too."

"I'm glad you could make it."

"Me, too!" Eden said with a big grin. She hugged Baleigh and whispered, "You doing okay?"

"I am."

"Good. Let's get you settled, and then I want to introduce you to Milos. He's Nick's cousin and chef. Be warned, he's a bit of a flirt, but he's harmless." She laughed and walked with her over to the table where they would later eat. The diner had been rearranged. There was now a large round table covered with a white cloth positioned in the middle of the room. From the amount of dishes at each setting, this was to be a multi-course dinner.

"Would you care for a drink? We have wine, soda, tea, and water."

"Wine please."

"Be right back."

Baleigh looked around the diner. Even with the change in the room, it still had that warm, friendly vibe it had the first time she ate there.

"Here you go." Lisa handed her a glass. Eden stood next to her holding a bottle of wine and filled each of their glasses.

"Here's to a night of good food and good fun."

"I'll second that. I love coming here when they get ready to change the menu. You're going to love the food," Lisa told her. "Eden, let's go introduce her to Milos."

Baleigh walked with Eden and Lisa into the kitchen. Milos was from Crete. He was very handsome with olive skin, curly black hair, and dark brown eyes. He stood about five foot five inches and had the swagger of one who was confident in his craft, and in who he was as a man. He was funny, and he flirted with them as he fed them samples of some of the appetizers he'd prepared. They stayed in the kitchen drinking wine and talking with Milos until he told them it was time for him to serve the meal.

As they sat down at the table, all but four seats were filled. The two seats next to her were empty. She assumed they'd probably be taken by Milos, his wife Ana, and their two teenage children who were helping them serve the meal. When the wine was poured, Nick thanked them for coming.

"I'd also like to welcome Baleigh. This is a tradition of sorts for us. Every time we get ready to change the menu, we use it as an excuse to get together, eat, and drink."

"We don't need an excuse to drink, but it's hard to pass up free food," Jay chimed in. They laughed, and Milos and Ana took their seats at the table next to Eden as the first course came out. The dinner was excellent. The conversation was filled with stories about each course, jokes, and funny stories about previous gatherings. Baleigh found herself in the midst of a very pleasant evening even though she had initially dreaded the thought of spending it with Sam's friends and being the only one at the table without a significant other.

When it came time for dessert, Milos and Ana got up and returned to the kitchen—Milos to plate the dessert, and Ana to prepare the coffee.

"Nick, this was good. Thanks for the invite."

"You're welcome," he responded with a sincere smile. "We're really glad you could come." As the others at the table continued to talk amongst themselves, Lisa mentioned that Baleigh was going to do some consulting for her and Jay.

"I didn't know you were a consultant," Eden said. "Funny, out of everything we've talked about over the last few weeks, we didn't talk too much about work. I used to be in the consulting business as well. My areas of expertise were bars and restaurants. I met Nick at a trade show."

"One look at me, a taste of Milos' baklava, and she was mine, much to the dismay of her co-worker who had been trying to get her to mix business with pleasure," Nick added.

"Nick likes to think it was his charm, but it was the baklava," Eden smirked.

Nick pulled his phone out, looked at it, rose, excused himself, and walked towards the kitchen. Milos and Ana returned to the room. He helped Ana pour the coffee as their children served the dessert. They'd also placed coffee and dessert at the empty places next to Baleigh. She thought maybe the teenagers were joining them for dessert. *No*, she was wrong, that was not the case. She heard voices, and one of them sounded suspiciously like Sam. Except it couldn't be Sam because he was supposed to be out of town. She looked at Eden, who was adding sugar to her coffee and avoiding eye contact with her. She then turned to glare at Lisa and Jay. Both looked back at her as if nothing was wrong.

"I hope we're not too late," Sam said as he walked into the dining room behind Nick, followed by Jesse. Sam sat down next to Baleigh. She looked at him and felt the immediate return of her anger. Her anger was so intense, that she couldn't speak. Sam reached over to grab her hand, and she snatched it away from him and started to get up from her chair. "Wait." He took her hand again.

"Let go of my hand," she hissed.

"No."

"Let. Go. Of. My. Hand," she repeated angrily.

"No."

Baleigh was getting more pissed by the second. She stood up and reached over with her other hand, intending to slap him in an effort to free herself. He grabbed that hand also. She began to struggle to try and get her hands loose.

"We can do this all damn night, Baleigh. I'm not letting your stubborn ass go until you hear me out."

"No, we won't, because I'm leaving!" Baleigh jerked away from him and was about to grab her purse when she noticed everyone staring at her and Sam, not even pretending they weren't listening. "What are y'all looking at?!"

"Aww, Baleigh, don't be that way, we were only trying to help," Nick said apologetically.

"And setting me up like this is your way of helping?"

"Come on, Bibi, hear the man out. If you still want to leave after that, I'll take you home." This came from Jay.

Baleigh glared at Sam and remained silent. Taking her silence as a yes, he took her arm and steered her away from the group.

"Hey! Where are you going?" Lisa asked.

"To get some privacy," Sam replied.

"But we can't hear you if you leave the room," Eden called after them.

"And…?" Sam looked at each of them before leaving the room with Baleigh.

"She seems pretty angry. Should I be worried?" Jesse asked, concern in his gaze as he watched the couple leave.

Lisa gave Jesse's shoulder a comforting squeeze. "It'll be okay."

"What you should worry about is whether or not they wait to get home before they have make-up sex." Eden laughed. They all stared at her. "What?" she asked. "I think Sam will be able to get Baleigh to take him back. And when he does, they're gonna need a release for all that emotional energy. Just saying."

Milos, who had been watching with amusement, chimed in. "I don't know Baleigh, but I agree with Eden. Jesse, we'll give you a ride home so you can avoid any potential embarrassment." This was met with a chorus of laughter.

Sam guided Baleigh to the other side of the restaurant away from the listening ears of their well-meaning but nosy friends.

"Say what you came to say so I can leave."

"Alright. I'm sorry. You trusted me with your heart, and I hurt you. I love you, and I don't want to be with anyone but you. *Please* forgive me."

"That's it? That's all you've got to say?! What about Kacey?!"

"What about her?"

"I can't be in a relationship with you and the connection you'll have with her. Once she has your baby, she's going to be in your life forever."

"No, she won't. She's not pregnant. If you would've taken my calls, listened to my messages, or read my texts, you would have known that by now." He loosened his grip on her hands and began to caress them. "Please, Baleigh. I need you. I don't want to spend the rest of my life without you."

"No." Baleigh lowered her head. "I can't do this again."

"What do you mean you can't do *this* again? Do what? Run away at the first sign of a problem? Because that's what you did," Sam asked angrily. He closed his eyes and pinched the bridge of his nose as he took a deep breath to calm himself. Opening his eyes, he looked at her. "I love you, Baleigh, and you left me. Rather than stay with me, you chose to leave. You let your past dictate our future."

"No, that's not what I did! It's not that I have a problem with you having a child with another woman. I mean, you have Jesse, and you've been a great father to him. You've been hands-on and very involved in his life. But Jesse is a grown man. It's not that I didn't want to be with you. I know you would've been just as great of a father to that child had there been one. I just didn't want to have to deal with Kacey and all of what would come with it. At this stage of my life, I don't want that. I just want you and me. At the time, I felt it was better to end things there since that was not to be." Baleigh lowered her head as the tears began to flow. "I was sad when I first left because I thought after all that happened, my heart still ended up bruised and broken. Then, I got angry because in opening myself up to you, I realized that it had been worth the risk, and I ruined everything by running. I was also angry at you for letting me leave." Smiling weakly, she sniffed and said, "I know that last part sounds stupid and selfish, but it's how I felt."

"Hey, watch it. That's my woman you're calling stupid and selfish." Sam smiled, moved toward her, and placed a kiss on her forehead before placing a hand underneath her chin to raise her head. "Please, babe."

Looking into Sam's eyes, she saw sincerity and hope. She felt her resolve weaken as tears began to flow in earnest. She took a deep breath and slowly nodded her head.

"I need to hear you say the words."

"Yes, Sam." He gently wiped her tears, then he kissed her. What started as a quick kiss deepened until they both seemed to forget where they were.

"Ahem," Jay cleared his throat. "Ease up you two. There are children present." Sam and Baleigh broke apart and looked back across the room at their friends, him smiling broadly and her slightly embarrassed. Everyone laughed.

"I'm glad you forgave me." Sam gave Baleigh a lingering kiss on the lips and led them both back to the table where they joined the others. "Because if you hadn't, I was going to have to resort to Plan B."

"Plan B? What was that?" she asked.

"You don't want to know." Jesse dug into the dessert in front of him. "But it could've resulted in him possibly getting arrested, you getting a restraining order against him, or both."

"I can't believe you all set me up like this." She looked at each person around the table.

"We had no choice. You're stubborn as hell. Once you get set on something, it almost takes a miracle to get you to change your mind." Lisa pointed her dessert fork at Baleigh as she spoke.

"That's not true!"

"Yes, it is. Be quiet and eat your dessert 'cause now you're just lying to yourself." Lisa laughed. Baleigh turned to Sam who was smiling, lifting a forkful of the chocolate pistachio dessert towards her. She smiled and opened her mouth to accept his offer.

"Thanks," she said.

"No, thank you."

Jesse, having finished his dessert, rose from the table. "How about we take a family picture?" He reached down and took his camera and tripod out of the bag on the floor near his feet. He set up the camera, grabbed the remote, and sat back down. "Okay, everybody. Look at the camera." Instead of looking at the camera, they turned to look at Sam and Baleigh. Confused, Baleigh returned their stare.

"The camera is over there," Baleigh said, pointing towards the tripod where the camera was mounted.

Sam got out of his chair and got down on one knee. "They're looking at us because they don't want to miss this." He took a small, black box from his pocket and grabbed her hand. "Baleigh Emerson, I love you. I was serious when I said that I didn't want to spend the rest of my life without you. The only way I know to do that is if you become my wife. Will you marry me?" Baleigh was stunned.

She nodded "Yes!"

Sam placed the ring on her finger. He stood up, pulled her out of the chair, and gave her a long, hot kiss.

"Damn it, Sam! I told you there were children present!" Hearing that, they separated, laughing.

"I got all of that on film in case you want to watch it later. In the meantime, how about that group photo?" Jesse got them into position facing the camera. "On the count of three…"

<u>Epilogue</u>

Two years later

Baleigh was doing some last-minute arranging before their guests arrived. She and Sam were having a party to celebrate Jesse finishing grad school. The original plan had been to rent out a venue, but Jesse wanted something small and low-key. The guest list included his mother and stepfather, his grandparents, Nick, Eden, Lisa, Jay and his parents, Milos and his family, and Rachel, the young lady he'd met in Fallston. They'd stayed in contact after the wedding and had become exclusive. She relocated to the area last year.

Baleigh stood, looking at the pictures that were placed around the room and on the mantle of the fireplace. Some of them were from the weekend she and Sam had first met. Others were pictures Jesse had taken during Jay and Lisa's wedding festivities in Colorado and the night Sam had proposed to her at Nick's restaurant. Her favorite picture was of her and Sam at the botanical gardens on the day of their wedding. Their ceremony was held in the gardens, surrounded by family and friends. It had been a beautiful day and one of the happiest of her life.

Sam walked up behind her and kissed her temple. "We should make sure we get a group picture tonight." She turned in his arms and faced him.

"I think Jesse would like that." She wrapped her arms around his neck and kissed him back.

"We have about two hours before our guests arrive. You know what I'd like?" He looked at her, his eyes sparkling with mischief. He leaned down, whispering in her ear in explicit detail what he wanted, then trailed his lips from her ear to her neck.

"I'd like that, too," Baleigh sighed.

He grabbed her hand and led her down the hallway toward their bedroom.

Acknowledgements

Thank you, God, for giving me this story and the courage to publish it. It has been an interesting and exciting journey. I'd like to thank the following people: John N.—the information you shared during a volunteer event was instrumental in getting me to give serious consideration to writing. Tori L.—best hype woman ever as well, sister-cousin and friend.

April B.—the best Bestie ever! Nickigh J.—thanks for the good talks. Devany T.—good friend and travel buddy. One More Glance Editing, All That's Wright LLC., Tiff Writes Romance, and GracePoint Publishing. To Tenth Muse Enterprises LLC Publishing and Brand Strategist—that first writing class led to this book. Looking forward to see what's next. Last but definitely not least, I would like to give a heartfelt thanks to the authors in the IR romance community who encouraged me, answered my questions, connected me to resources to help bring my writing to life, etc. Your kindness is greatly appreciated.

About the Author

Harper Black's curiosity about the world was stirred at an early age as she sought to live a life far different from that of Laverne and Shirley, the TV sitcom heroines of her hometown Milwaukee, Wisconsin. That curiosity, a desire to get a college education, and a sense of adventure, led Harper to enlist in the U.S. Navy. Black's military career took her to destinations that were both intrepid and romantic, embarking on a journey to achieve her professional goals while navigating the ebbs and flows of international romance. Her travels included memorable experiences in Scotland, Italy, and Egypt as a single woman, investigating the dating scenes in global cities, open to the possibility of meeting her life partner. In her stories, Harper crafts romantic adventures that reflect diverse cultures and encourages each of us to follow our desire for true love wherever it takes us. She currently writes from her home in northern California.

Website: www.HarperBlackWrites.com

Instagram: @harperblack10writes

www.ingramcontent.com/pod-product-compliance
Lightning Source LLC
Chambersburg PA
CBHW031018160726
47991CB00005B/1778